Rave reviews for the novels of
Carly Phillips

CROSS MY HEART

"Who doesn't love a reunion of long-lost loves?
Add a diabolical villain, as Carly Phillips does,
and you have everything you need for a beach read."
—*Columbus Dispatch*

"Smart, engrossing and totally addictive! *Cross My Heart*
is a definite must-have in this season's beach bag."
—*www.FreshFiction.com*

SUMMER LOVIN'

"Phillips's light touch assures a happy ending
to this diverting beach read."
—*Publishers Weekly*

"A funny and touching family drama."
—*Romantic Times BOOKreviews*

"A fun, yet emotional story. A story that will keep you
hooked with its kooky, yet charming characters."
—*Romance Reviews Today*

What's steamier than a New York City summer?
Carly Phillips's Hot series!

HOT ITEM

"Saving her best for last, Phillips wraps up
her jocular Hot Zone trilogy...."
—*Publishers Weekly*

"Phillips has penned a charming, fast-paced
contemporary romp-through-the-sheets."
—*Booklist*

"*Hot Item* is a winner."
—*Romance Reviews Today*

HOT NUMBER

"A veteran romance author who climbed to star status in Harlequin's Temptation line, Phillips is certain to capture a new bank of fans with the fresh venue and stylish dialogue featured in this perky series."
—*Publishers Weekly*

"*Hot Number* is a fun, sexy read. For everyone who has ever wished to turn the head of a guy, this book definitely allows you that fantasy while giving you a satisfying love story. Ms. Phillips has proven herself more than capable of delivering stories that touch your heart and your funnybone."
—*In the Library Reviews*

"In the follow-up to last year's *Hot Stuff*, Phillips once again dives into the high pressure world of sports. Micki and Damian each have quite a few issues to resolve, which adds spice to an already volatile mixture."
—Jill M. Smith, *Romantic Times BOOKreviews* (4 stars)

"Carly Phillips hits a home run with the fun, yet touching *Hot Number*."
—Jennifer Bishop, *Romance Reviews Today*

HOT STUFF

"This breezy book will likely score a touchdown with readers looking for sexy thrills and instant gratification."
—*Publishers Weekly*

"This first book in The Hot Zone trilogy shines with Phillips' trademark sizzle and sensuality. She delivers strong, appealing characters while exploring the dynamics of families—what brings them together and what draws them apart. The ending emotionally satisfies and gives readers a tantalizing peek at the romantic quandaries awaiting the rest of the family."
—*Romantic Times BOOKreviews* (4 stars)

"*Hot Stuff* is a surefire hit."
—Jennifer Bishop, *Romance Reviews Today*

CARLY PHILLIPS
SIMPLY
Scandalous

HQN™

ISBN-13: 978-0-373-77288-9
ISBN-10:   0-373-77288-2

SIMPLY SCANDALOUS

Copyright © 2000 by Karen Drogin

www.HQNBooks.com

Printed in U.S.A.

SIMPLY
Scandalous

CHAPTER ONE

"TARGET AT ONE O'CLOCK."

Logan Montgomery listened to his eighty-year-old grandmother and groaned. "You've been watching James Bond again, Gran."

"Just Sean Connery. That Pierce Brosnan is too new and the other one is a pansy. He wouldn't know how to please a real woman if she bit him on the—"

"*Gran!*" Startled, Logan shot a glance at his grandmother.

An impish gleam lit her knowing gaze. She'd learned to use shock value to her advantage, he thought wryly. "I think that's enough."

"You never used to be a prude."

He stifled a laugh and chose to warn the irrepressible older woman instead. "And you never used to go so far. Better watch yourself."

The white-haired woman gave an unrefined,

unladylike snort. "If you aren't careful you'll end up a stuffed shirt like your father."

"With your influence? Not a chance." He drank from a glass of hundred-dollar champagne, tasting bubbles and little else. Damn waste of money. A cold beer would taste a hell of a lot better, especially on such an unusually hot and balmy May afternoon. "So tell me why you summoned me to the annual Garden Gala."

He'd hoped he could ignore the formal invitation, hand-delivered to his house, as it had been hand-delivered to dozens of others. Although the Garden Gala was as much a part of Montgomery tradition as baseball was a part of spring, Logan didn't feel the same sense of anticipation for this event. His grandmother, Emma, was a different story. He adored her.

"Because of her." His grandmother waved a wrinkled finger in front of his eyes. "Over there by the Dogwood tree. She catered this whole party herself. Talent personified."

Logan narrowed his gaze. He couldn't see much besides the overwhelming sea of floral prints on the female guests and the stark black-and-white uniforms worn by the help. "All I see is a bunch of penguins," Logan muttered.

"I believe waiter or waitress is the politically correct term," Emma said.

"Couldn't you get the judge to relax the dress code for God's sake? These poor people look like they're attending a formal wedding, not serving cocktails on a spring day."

He liked parties as much as the next guy but this uptight excuse for a gathering wasn't the way he'd choose to spend a Saturday afternoon.

"Your father has his *standards*," Emma said in her haughtiest voice, in imitation of her son, Judge Montgomery. "He believes the help should dress as such. Ridiculous," she muttered. "The man ought to come into the twenty-first century. Anyway, enough about Edgar for now. Look around. What else do you see?"

Logan took two steps to the right so he could see around a ridiculous-looking parasol held by one of his mother's friends, to protect her skin from the nonexistent sun and impending rain.

"Well?" A bony elbow nudged Logan in the ribs.

He looked once more and was rewarded by what he saw at the elaborate bar set up in front of the pool house, on the perfectly manicured lawn—a delectable-looking creature in uniform. She stepped around the bar and into full view. The clouds had begun rolling in but this woman radiated pure sunshine. Not even the standard waitress uniform looked ordinary on her supple curves.

She reached over to clean the bar of used glasses, and Logan was treated to a backside view that was just as enticing. Black running shoes, obviously worn for comfort, and black tights with a vertical seam ran up the length of her well-toned legs. As she reached forward to sweep the top of the bar with a damp rag, the hem on her black miniskirt inched higher. He stepped closer in time to catch a hint of lace peeking beneath the black hem. Interest replaced curiosity and the temperature outside hitched up a notch. So did strategic body parts. He stuck one finger inside the constricting collar of his white shirt, giving himself some breathing room.

She rose to her full height, which wasn't much. Petite, with blond hair pinned on top of her head, she couldn't have been more than five foot three. Considering he had one sister who had traipsed more friends through the house than he could count on both hands, Logan considered himself an expert on all things female.

And this female intrigued him. His gaze traveled over her form-fitting white blouse, which was buttoned to her chin but failed to hide well-rounded breasts, lingered on the belt cinched over a small waist and settled on the white socks pulled over the sheer stockings. She wasn't a typical waitress by any means.

Didn't matter if he looked from the bottom up, or the top down, he liked what he saw. A smile edged the corners of his mouth.

"Quit drooling and tell me what you see."

"A damn sexy penguin," he muttered.

"Call her what you want," Emma said, resigned. "She's the solution to your problems."

"Didn't know I had any." Another glance as she swung back around the bar and he grinned. If he had a problem, he sure wouldn't mind this woman being his solution.

"Do you want to put an end to Montgomery expectations or do you want your parents and their big-money friends to keep hounding you to run for public office? No peace, no quiet. And bye-bye low profile job at the public defender's office. Once next Saturday is over, your life will be out of your hands."

"You don't have to sound like you're enjoying this," Logan muttered. But instinct told him his grandmother wasn't just trying to shock him now. Emma lived in this mausoleum along with both of Logan's parents. She was privy to details Logan wasn't and shared that information willingly. He turned his attention back to the older woman.

"You can keep telling them no thank you." She patted her perfect bun into place as she spoke. Not even the humidity touched Emma's coiffure. "But your daddy's been stubborn as a mule and insistent on having his own way since he was in dirty diapers."

He stifled the urge to laugh again. She didn't need an audience. "You've really got to watch your mouth."

"Nonsense. Age gives me the right to say and do whatever youth prevented me from saying or doing. The expression is young and stupid, not old and stupid."

Logan grinned. "I know now why Dad wants you in a home." He gazed at the outspoken woman who had given him and his sister their only source of love and affection growing up. In their best interests, she'd undermined his parents' efforts at making their children clones of their own public-perfect selves. She'd accomplished her goal with his sister.

But with Logan, the only son, things had been more difficult. Though he'd traveled his own path, many of his choices—college, law school and his stint as district attorney—had paralleled his father's.

No one believed he intended to chart his own

destiny. Not even the past two years spent working on the wrong side of the tracks, at the public defender's office, swayed his family's beliefs. To all the Montgomerys, Logan was the next generation, destined to follow in past footsteps.

Except to his beloved grandmother. To Emma, Logan was the grandson she'd raised, a man with his own beliefs. He turned his attention back to what she'd said minutes earlier. "Okay, let me have it. What's happening on Saturday?" he asked.

"I thought you'd never ask." She nudged Logan, urging him to walk with her. Resigned, he followed the sound of the crinkling taffeta of her long daydress until she reached her destination. Emma gestured across the patio to where his father was holding court. "In one week your father and his conservative cronies plan on announcing your candidacy for mayor of our fair city. Hampshire needs some young blood and you've been handpicked. Perfect son of the esteemed Montgomery family on his first stepping-stone to even higher office."

"Never happen," he said.

"That's right and I'll tell you why. We're going to publicly disgrace you. Free you to live life outside the realm."

He drew a deep breath and forcibly stopped himself from rolling his eyes at her theatrics. "I don't need scandal to free myself from the family. They can talk politics until doomsday, but without a willing candidate, they've got nothing." And Logan was completely unwilling.

"You drove all the way out to Hampshire, so at least hear me out."

As usual, the older woman had a point. Besides, he had no place else to be and the view from this angle was good.

Logan folded his arms over his chest. "You mentioned a plan," he prodded. "So how can she save me?" He pointed to the blonde across the way.

Emma nodded. "You need a public trashing and who better to ruin your reputation than a woman born into poverty with a family history of prostitution behind her?"

He choked on champagne bubbles. "You're exaggerating." He glanced at Emma's target.

She'd left the covering of the bar and now tread with a light step, gliding among the guests, talking quietly with the help serving hors d'oeuvres. Her air of authority set her apart from the other hired help. So did the miniskirt she wore in place of the black pants favored by the rest of the waitresses. A black bow tie nestled below her chin, accentuating her heart-shaped face. How had he missed that before?

"She owns Pot Luck, the caterers. She doesn't attend every event her company caters, but I insisted she run this one."

"Of course you did," he muttered.

"She's a woman after my own heart. Remember the charm school the cops closed down last year?"

"Vaguely. I was out of state." He'd graduated from Columbia Law School and snagged a job at the Manhattan district attorney's office, working there until Emma's mild heart attack this past year brought him home. He wanted more time with his family. Other than his sister, Grace, with whom he'd bunked in Manhattan, Emma was the only family who counted.

"Well, she and her sister," Emma said, pointing to the caterer, "inherited that business. Turns out the previous owner, her uncle, was operating a call-girl service in disguise."

"But she wasn't involved."

"Well, no, but it's family scandal. And to make things even better, she used to work for them when she was in college." His grandmother clapped her hands in growing excitement.

"She was a *prostitute?*"

"Bite your slandering tongue. She taught classes for the testosterone impaired. All on the up-and-up. But think of your parents' reaction if you brought home a woman whose family had dabbled in prostitution. A woman who instructed the single man on how to score."

Certain she had done no such thing, Logan refused to touch that outrageous comment. "I don't bring women home," he said instead.

Why should he? His parents would take it as a sign the prodigal son was ready to settle down. Logan couldn't say he wasn't itching for steady companionship. He was. He couldn't say he didn't long for someone to come home to at the end of the day. He wanted that, too. But he'd yet to meet a woman who interested him enough to forsake all others, let alone one he could imagine looking at across the dinner table each and every night for the rest of his natural life.

"You would if you met the right one," his grandmother said, with a gleam in her eyes that alarmed him.

The old lady had an agenda. Logan only wished he knew more. Just because Emma was admitting her scheme aloud didn't mean she was revealing all.

He knew her too well to be anywhere near

complacent, but he decided to humor her for now. "My social life is plenty full, Gran. Too full to settle for just one female out of the bunch."

His social life was full, all right. Full of renovation and restoration. Logan was busy, just not busy playing the field. But a white lie wouldn't hurt anyone, least of all Emma, who needed to believe Logan was happy and on the lookout for the future Mrs. Montgomery.

While he met, dated and appreciated females as much as any man, he didn't see a long-term relationship in his future. The women he met at the P.D.'s office and the opposing counsel he ran into around the courthouse cared more for what the Montgomery name could do for them than in Logan himself. Same for the women in his parents' illustrious social circle. They sought only to marry and keep their steady income streaming in. All were disappointed and disinterested once they discovered Logan lived off his salary and kept himself isolated from the family legacy.

A marriage for the sake of appearances, like the one his parents shared, didn't interest him. No one benefited from a loveless union—especially not the requisite number of children, born only for show. Children raised by servants and ignored by their parents.

"Open your eyes, son. You never know what's in front of you. Now, as I was saying about your father and his mayoral ideas. If making your point in private doesn't work, we can always resort to the headlines. Judge Montgomery's Son Dating Ex-Hooker. Not that I'm in favor of that approach, mind you—Catherine deserves better." She pointed to the woman in the corner.

At least now she had a name. He'd need one if he wanted to get to know her better.

"You know how the papers exaggerate about sex," Emma said. "You'll be a dropout candidate before you know it."

He let out a groan. Humoring her was getting more difficult. "I hate to break it to you, Gran, but sex scandals don't affect approval ratings anymore."

Emma shrugged. "Maybe not but I can see you're interested. So go for it with Cat and get caught. My money says the embarrassment will be enough. Your father will call off the campaign."

Logan shook his head. "You really do have an overactive imagination. There's no reason to go that far. A press conference minus the candidate will take care of any expectations."

"And how would that affect your job at the public defender's office? I happen to know it's a first step toward opening your own law office down on the docks."

"Both are my business and as much as I appreciate your concern, I can handle my life without help."

As if on cue, a large hand slapped Logan on the shoulder. "Good to see you, son. I knew you wouldn't miss a chance to mingle with your supporters."

In a move she'd perfected over the years, his grandmother raised an eyebrow and nodded her head, as if to say, *I told you so.*

He met his father's gaze. "Of course not. These people are very important." To Emma, Logan added silently, which was the only reason he'd chosen to attend.

His father puffed out his chest and beamed, obviously misconstruing Logan's agreement. Logan didn't bother to explain. The judge would never listen.

"I'm glad you agree. Now you've got to learn the art of working a room," Edgar said.

"What room?" Logan asked, deliberately playing dumb. He glanced at the sky and the clouds that had been steadily rolling in. "I thought this was an outdoor garden party, not a political fund-raiser."

"I like your sense of humor, son."

Behind the judge's back, Emma caught Logan's attention with a wave. She rolled her eyes and they shared a silent laugh at the judge's single-mindedness.

"Glad you're amused," Logan muttered.

"Yes, but you know as well as I do that behind every event there is a purpose," the older man said. "The fact that you showed up for this is telling." He adjusted the lapels of his jacket.

Logan waited a beat before walking around and placing an arm around his grandmother's shoulder. "The only thing my appearance should tell you is I wouldn't miss one of Emma's extravaganzas. Beyond that, I have no purpose or hidden agenda."

He gave the older woman a loving squeeze. Her frailty stunned him a moment before he reassured himself. Behind the aging body lay an agile mind and a generous spirit.

"I promised him a good time, something you've never learned how to have." An irreverent gleam sparkled in the older woman's gaze.

The judge shot his mother a warning look then faced Logan once more. "We need to talk."

Logan studied his father. With his dark double-breasted suit and air of authority, Judge Montgomery appeared every inch the man in control of his domain. Too bad for him Logan no longer lived within that realm, nor could he be manipulated. "There's nothing to discuss."

The judge shook his head. "I want what's best for you, son, and that means putting you in public office."

"Placing me in office is what's best for *you*. You want me to carry on the political tradition. I want to live my own life."

"You're young." He clapped Logan on the shoulder. "You'll come around."

Logan raised an eyebrow. "You're probably right. After all, I bought my house even after you put a down payment on a penthouse apartment in Boston. I took the P.D.'s job even after you pulled strings at Fitch and Fitzwater, the leading firm downtown." He shrugged. "I suppose if you hold your breath long enough, I might come around after all."

Edgar narrowed his eyes. "This is your influence," the judge said to his mother.

"If so, I'm proud of him. And you should be, too," Emma said. "Shame on you, Edgar. I raised you better than this."

"Logan, see to it your grandmother gets some rest. She's cranky. We'll talk more later." He issued his commands and, without awaiting a response, he turned and strode toward his guests.

"He's determined," Emma said.

"I'm more determined." But Logan was also tired of the battle. A part of him wished he didn't have to fight his father for every step he took in his own life.

"Still think you don't need my help?" Emma asked.

"I love you for your concern but I can handle the judge alone."

"But her kind of help would be so much more fun," his grandmother said, her gaze shifting from him.

Logan followed her glance at the woman standing on a chair, adjusting a speaker, and he had to agree. Still, no matter how tempting, he wouldn't use an innocent woman as a pawn in his family's game.

But that didn't mean he couldn't pursue this attraction and get to know her for his own reasons. As Emma had probably predicted, she fascinated him in a way few women did and he wanted to know why. He placed the champagne glass down on a passing server's tray.

"I'm here if you need backup," Emma said.

He kissed the older woman's weathered cheek. "I'm sure I can handle it," he said wryly. He glanced across the lawn to where Catherine had settled back into bartender mode.

She handled the bottles and glasses with ease. Logan grinned at the sight. One of the cocktail waitresses paused and whispered something in her ear. Catherine bolted from behind the bar and headed toward the house. Without her presence, the bar loomed as empty and boring as the party had minutes earlier.

Logan sighed, seeing opportunity vanish at least for the moment.

"She's got the goodies," Emma said. "She'll be back."

"I believe drinks or liquor is the politically correct term these days." He couldn't help but needle his grandmother.

His gaze followed Catherine's retreating form. The well-shaped bottom and trim waist were a sight to behold before she disappeared inside the open French doors.

Emma cleared her throat. "From your perspective I'd say she's got the goodies," she said with a laugh.

He chuckled. "I'd say you were right."

A SEXY MAN HAD been watching Catherine for the last fifteen minutes. He had dark hair, model-like looks, and a penetrating stare that made her muscles weak and her heart flutter. She couldn't imagine what sparked his interest when there were dozens of other women at the party. Female guests dressed in silky dresses and flowing chiffon skirts, beautiful women with perfectly manicured nails and hair straight from the beauty salon.

Catherine's sneakers—comfortable shoes for a day of working on her feet—squeaked as she crossed the gleaming marble floors. She cringed and kept going. Years had passed since she had felt this…inadequate, she thought, coming up with the right word. She glanced down at her working outfit, the same one she wore to any party her company catered. Instead of feeling comfortable in her own skin, she felt out of place and transported back in time, to when she and her sister had been the Luck girls from the wrong side of the tracks.

Catherine shook her head and raised her chin a notch. There was no sense denying it. The rich were different. But Catherine had worked too hard and come too far to let insecurities hit her now. She'd survive this party. As long as the threatening rain held off…and her chef didn't bail out.

She and her company Pot Luck couldn't afford the disaster. With Kayla, her business partner and sister, pregnant and under doctor's orders to stay in bed, Catherine was handling more than usual. Between doing the food prep work for today, substituting as bartender, overseeing along with her manager and planning upcoming bookings, Catherine was overworked and stressed. As soon as the temperature warmed, people clamored to organize outdoor events and Pot Luck was booked solid.

She couldn't complain about being busy, but she did long for future days when all they would have to cater was full-scale parties like this one. But for now Pot Luck accommodated any request—from complete party packages, to hors d'oeuvres only, to simple decorations and party favors. Some day, once their reputation was more firmly established and the bank account posted a hefty surplus, they could be more discriminating—and Catherine could make more use of her culinary background as well. After this event, someday could arrive faster than she'd ever imagined.

The Montgomery party had been a coup and Catherine had no problem with rearranging her schedule to accommodate Emma Montgomery.

Success here would mean referrals to the wealthiest people and most prestigious companies in Hampshire. She wouldn't allow anything to ruin this chance, especially not a temperamental chef who was her oldest friend.

She entered the state-of-the-art kitchen where stainless steel and chrome gleamed from every corner of the room. "Nick, you're a hit!" Catherine made her way around a long center island and placed a kiss on his clean-shaven cheek.

"The duck isn't cold," he denied, whacking at a large chunk of meat with a knife.

"I never said it was. The guests love the hors d'oeuvres. They're going to spread your name from here to downtown Boston."

Another loud whack sounded against the cutting board. "I'm already famous in Boston. I don't need to take abuse because your help can't get in here fast enough to serve hot food." Beneath his anger and frustration, she recognized the concern and warning. Someone had been complaining about the temperature of the food. She cringed. She'd take care of her lazy help, but first she had to calm the chef.

Catherine glanced at his exaggerated pout. She'd grown up with Nick. She knew when to worry and when a word or two would smooth things over. She snuck a peek inside the large oven and inhaled an enticing aroma. "This smells heavenly. I don't know another chef who can create the way you do." She returned to his side. "The food is *almost* as good-looking as you are."

The knife slammed into the wooden board again and he glanced up, dark eyes narrowed. "Don't try to flatter me, Cat. It won't work." His gaze settled on her for the first time and he touched her cheek with one hand. "You're red."

"The day is so overcast I forgot the sunscreen." Catherine shrugged. "Besides we can't all bronze like you."

"You're fair. You ought to be more careful."

She rolled her eyes. For as far back as she could remember, Nick had looked out for her. He had classic Mediterranean looks and most women would have snatched him up at the slightest chance. Not Catherine. Lovers came and went; best friends were for life. "If you're so worried about me, stop yelling at the help."

"They're incompetent."

"I'll talk to them. I promise."

"It's a start. What's going on out there? Is Mr. Right mingling among the guests?"

"Back off, Nick. Just because you're engaged doesn't mean everyone else wants the brass ring."

Catherine had no desire to have this conversation with Nick yet again. "Look, the bartender never showed. I'm already pulling double duty and I can't afford to have the help leave in tears. Now will you lay off the girls?"

He raised an eyebrow. "If you promise to use this party as an opportunity. There are men out there, Cat. All types of men. Tall and thin, fat and balding, rich and richer. Take your pick."

A sexy stranger with dark hair and compelling eyes filled her mind. She pushed the thought aside. Before she'd entered this immense house filled with elegant women, she'd believed herself over the painful memories associated with her lower-class upbringing. Just working this party, being surrounded by delicate perfection, brought the painful memories back full force.

Sexual attraction from across a crowded room meant nothing when she and the stranger were obviously worlds apart. "You know the guests here are way out of my league," she told her friend.

"Only because *you* think so, not because it's true. You spend too much time alone."

Catherine shrugged. "At least the company's good."

Nick groaned.

"Is it my fault every guy I've dated isn't *the one?*" Catherine had yet to meet a man worth risking her heart for. Despite what Nick thought, she certainly wouldn't find him here.

"You walk away before any guy can prove himself. Take me, for instance."

She rolled her eyes. "I turned you down when we were sixteen and you survived." She glanced at her watch. "I promise nothing else will leave this kitchen cold. Back off the help?"

"Consider opening your eyes to the men out there," he countered.

"I'll consider it," she lied. "You're a prince," she called over her shoulder, adjusting her bow tie as she ran out of the kitchen.

She darted back outside, dismayed to find the clouds darker and heavier than five minutes before. The storm was rolling in faster than predicted. Winded from her sprint out of the kitchen, she rested her hands on the bar and closed her eyes. She inhaled deep, then exhaled, searching for calm. Too much hinged on getting through the rest of the afternoon without mishap.

A deep masculine drawl captured her attention. "So tell me what put the frown on that beautiful face." She'd never heard that voice before but her body reacted instantly. She knew who it belonged to. She just didn't know how in the world to handle him.

CHAPTER TWO

CATHERINE OPENED HER EYES and found herself staring into brown eyes the color of her morning coffee, after she'd added the cream. She forced a confident smile. "What can I get for you?" she asked.

"The specialty of the house. What's yours?" A sexy near-perfect grin blindsided her and her breath caught in a hitch.

Heavy awareness pulsed through her veins, a delicious accompaniment to the steady beat of the music in the background. Catherine wondered just how many women this man charmed with his good looks alone. Enough to make him dangerous, she thought.

He wore an Italian-cut suit as if he were to the manor born, and when those eyes captured hers, they didn't let go. Not even loud laughter from across the expanse of the outdoors caused his gaze to slide from hers.

She narrowed her eyes to gauge his preference but she wasn't a bartender by trade. She was merely substituting for her absent employee. Glancing at this man, she couldn't begin to guess his drink of choice. And though she could offer an interesting mix of cocktails, the general requests here had been for champagne or Mimosas and, somehow, she couldn't see him as a delicate-drink kind of guy. "Why don't you tell me what you had in mind?"

He leaned closer, elbows propped on the edge of the bar. His cologne smelled masculine and expensive, a sensual combination that reminded her of spice, temptation and trouble. "Something to cool me down and take the edge off the heat," he said.

The clouds had darkened to a stormy gray and a heavy breeze had already begun blowing off the nearby ocean, cutting back on the mugginess and heat. Catherine recognized his words for the come-on they were. Though she wanted to be flattered, she couldn't help but be disappointed as well.

"A splash of cold water would work just fine," she muttered. His eyes darkened subtly and she was appalled to realize she'd spoken the words out loud.

He grinned. "I could think of plenty of things that would work better."

He was too confident...too sexy. For all her bravado, Catherine wasn't as secure in herself as she liked the world to believe. Life's harsh realities had taught her not to trust in much—especially a tempting man who had charm and knew how to use it.

She glanced at him warily, deciding not to play. "Then how about a cold beer instead?"

His smile widened. "Now you're talking." He walked around the corner of the bar, seating himself on a stool—too close to Catherine's small work space. The width of a bar top separated them, but it wasn't much and certainly not enough. And with waitresses walking around passing out champagne off serving trays, the line for drinks had dwindled. She hadn't had a stray passerby in at least half an hour. They were alone.

She reached for one of the eclectic brews hand-picked by Judge Montgomery for the occasion and poured the man his drink. Placing the glass on a cocktail napkin, she slid the beer toward him.

"Join me?"

"I'm working," she said, as she wiped down the already shiny Lucite bar with a damp rag.

"I'll clear it with the management."

"*I'm* the management and I don't mix business and pleasure." Especially not when the risk would be greater than the pleasure...and if her tingling nerves and rising anticipation were any indication, she could just imagine how great the pleasure would be.

"Miss...Scotch and soda, if I may interrupt." The voice came from the opposite end of the bar.

Catherine grabbed on to the excuse and headed for the waiting guest. While she worked, she felt *his* heavy gaze burn right through her. Then, noticing a problem across the lawn, Catherine ran to avert disaster between her waitress and an intoxicated guest. She was used to the role of overseer and referee. But between the impending rain and the need for things to go well, this party had her completely stressed out.

To make matters worse, Judge Montgomery waylaid her on her way back to the bar. Though Emma led Catherine to believe she was in charge, her son left no doubt *he* was paying the bills. And he insisted that the waitresses needed to circulate more and that she shouldn't be fraternizing with the guests. Catherine had to swallow her pride as well as her comeback.

She saw no point in informing the man who

would pay for this event that *his* guest had come on to her. He wouldn't believe her if she had. Instead she bowed, escaped and got hold of her assistant to warn her to have a quick talk with all the help. Then she ran toward the bar. One thing she knew, she'd be happy when this day was over.

When she returned, her visitor sat in his same spot, arms folded across his broad chest. "You need a break," he informed her, a scowl on his face. Unfortunately it didn't do a thing to detract from his good looks.

"A break doesn't fit into my schedule."

"You've had an overwhelming day." He darted a glance to where she'd had her discussion with the host of the party. Emma might have employed her services, but Catherine had little doubt it was Judge Montgomery who held court over the world around him.

Her companion then patted a bar stool beside him. "Take a seat and pour your heart out," he said. "I'm a good listener." What looked like genuine concern etched his handsome features.

If she let him, he could seduce her with that concern. No doubt that was his goal, yet her body temperature inched higher despite his calculated manners. Or was it his warmth and seductive voice that heated her inside and out? "I think you have our roles reversed. *I'm* the bartender who's supposed to have the friendly ear."

He reached out, touching the silver earrings dangling from her ear. "But I'm not the one in need of a shoulder."

It was eerie how well he read her, Catherine thought. His strong hand heated her skin. She was in danger of sensual overload. Catherine shut her eyes against the tremor of awareness shooting through her veins. He affected her on more than the physical plane and that made the dynamics between them even more explosive.

She paused a beat. "I appreciate the thought but I shouldn't fraternize with the guests."

"You're doing a great job here. I wouldn't let anything—or anyone—get to you," he murmured.

Obviously he understood little about pleasing an employer and paying the bills.

"You're too old not to realize we all answer to a higher authority," she said wryly.

"But only when the authority is full of truth and honesty, not hot air," he said and grinned.

Catherine laughed despite herself. Judge Montgomery had made his displeasure clear. Catherine not only wanted success today, but she also wanted referrals galore. That wouldn't be happening if she spent the afternoon being verbally seduced by a sexy man way out of her league.

"I'm here to work," she reminded him.

"You know this party's a success. Ignore the man," he suggested. "Why let him tell you what to do?"

"Because he signs my paycheck. Besides," Catherine said, arching her eyebrow, "he told me to stay away from *you*. That's got to be good advice."

He shook his head. "Cynical is sad."

He spoke as if he'd read behind the words to her philosophy on life, love and dating in the new millennium. "It's honest. The only way I know how to be."

Dark eyes met hers. "I'll keep that in mind," he murmured.

He spoke sexy words laced with innuendo, Catherine reminded herself. Nothing more. She tipped her head back to meet his gaze. His nearly black hair had been slicked off his forehead in the latest style. Money and class. He possessed them both.

Behind him milled beautifully dressed women, women immaculately and properly groomed for the world he inhabited. She wondered why this man had chosen to hang out at the bar with the help. He wouldn't be interested in a woman way out of his social class with a shady family history.

She didn't know what he wanted, but she suspected he found her an interesting diversion. The thought tapped into her deepest fear—that not only was she like her mother, but she'd end up like her as well. Her mother had overdressed, overdone and had always fallen short. Always just been a woman with two daughters and too many responsibilities. A woman alone.

Feeling out of place here didn't help her frame of mind, merely heightened a fear Catherine normally suppressed. Unlike the wealthy Montgomerys, the Luck family had barely made ends meet, had lived on shop specials. And that was when things were good.

Although she lived a world apart from her roots, Catherine wasn't foolish enough to think a woman who once wore hand-me-downs and lived in the poorer sections of Boston had anything in common with this elegant and sexy man.

"Well, if you won't unburden yourself, we can go back to you doing your job. Another drink?" he asked. "Mine's gone flat." His deep voice vibrated too close to her ear. An unexpected tremor of excitement shimmied throughout her body.

"So has your routine," she said and grinned.

"Listen to the woman, sonny boy," Emma Montgomery said in her cultured voice.

"Go away. You're ruining my attempt at convincing the lady to give me a chance."

"Sounded to me like you were failing miserably."

Catherine laughed aloud.

"Eavesdroppers don't get the whole story. She was on the verge of agreeing to go for a drink when the party ended."

"I was?"

He stretched his arm over the back of the chair. "You were." His fingertips brushed her shoulder and she trembled. One drink. She met his heavy gaze and wondered, why not?

"I always knew my grandson had good taste." The older woman's words provided the answer.

It was one thing to have a drink with a good-looking guy, another to form illusions about a man who belonged to a family as wealthy as the Montgomerys. They would never accept her. Not on a bet. Not even if Emma Montgomery demanded it...and Catherine couldn't help doubting whether Emma would be as gracious toward Catherine regarding her grandson as she had been regarding business. She now understood Judge Montgomery's stern warning and obvious disdain. He didn't want her anywhere near his son.

Emma patted her hand. "Lovely party, Catherine. You exceeded my expectations."

A little while ago, Catherine would have agreed. After the last ten minutes, she had to wonder. And if there was anything Catherine hated, it was self-doubt and self-pity. She had to get·away from these people before she lost the one thing she treasured: her faith in herself. Hard-won faith.

She swallowed over the lump in her throat and glanced at her watch. Almost over. "I have to get back to work."

"You mean you don't want my company after all?" His eyes clouded. A wounded little boy look graced his chiseled features. If she wasn't careful, she'd believe she'd hurt his feelings. But the most she'd possibly offended was his pride. Protecting her heart was worth the sacrifice.

She watched Emma Montgomery's retreating, regal form. His grandmother. Catherine shook her head, disappointed. She turned back to the privileged son. "I'm not sure what you're after, but I can't provide it."

"Cut me some slack. Company's all I'm looking for. *Your* company."

She narrowed her eyes and she tried to gauge his sincerity. His gaze, once steady on her face, had slipped to her thigh. She glanced down. The hem of her miniskirt had bent up, exposing an expanse of skin hidden beneath the sheer black stockings. It wasn't much, but she'd revealed more than she'd wanted Prince Charming to see.

Company, her Aunt Fanny. She looked like an easy mark. Regret surged through her—it wasn't strong enough to douse the flame of desire he'd ignited, but she wasn't about to get burned. Or let him see he'd flustered her.

She left the skirt hem alone. "Sorry, I have other plans."

He shrugged and raised his hands in a gesture of defeat. "Okay. But you can't deny me another drink."

Because she was being paid to do the honors. She didn't appreciate the reminder. She shrugged. "I can't discriminate. It's my job."

"You wound me."

"You'll live." She sounded too breathless for her own liking. Yet he was right. She couldn't turn him away. Worse, she didn't want to.

But the sooner she gave him his drink, the sooner he'd be on his way. He wouldn't hang around her the rest of the afternoon being shot down. No matter how much she wished other-wise. "Okay, hotshot, tell me what I can get you."

LOGAN DOUBTED SHE WANTED to hear his real desire. Especially since it involved them both in a horizontal position with their naked bodies crushed together in a sweaty tangle beneath the sheets. Or in the pool cabana behind the bar.

"Hurry up. I need to refill the serving trays with champagne," she whispered.

Her warm breath tickled his ear. Her scent, an intoxicating oriental blend of spices, heated the rest of his senses. The mix of perfumes emanat-ing from the guests had grown heavy hours ago, hanging on the damp humid air. But Catherine's stood out, sexy and unique, like the lady herself.

His gaze dropped to her thigh. When she'd bristled the first time, he'd promised himself he wouldn't look again. But the hint of skin and the promise of what lay beneath was too much for a man to take.

She headed behind the bar, to obvious safety. Tapping her fingers impatiently against the top, she said, "I'm waiting."

"Patience," he murmured. "I want to make sure I get what I want." He had one shot at capturing her interest, at making her want to get to know him as badly as he wanted to know her.

"More likely you want an excuse to linger. What I don't know is why." Her green eyes shimmered with curiosity.

Which, Logan decided, was better than disgust or disinterest. He wanted to linger, all right. To sit here and drink in her blond beauty and sassy mouth. Logan eyed her warily, then reminded himself she may be female, but she wasn't a mind reader.

She might sense that he wanted more than her company—and she was right. But as much as he desired her, it was too soon for that to be an issue.

He'd have to take it slow. "What I want is something special," he said thinking aloud. "More than a plain old beer." He glanced down at her hands, noticing the blunt nails and clear polish for the first time. No fancy frills, colors or artifice to this woman, he thought and was more than pleased. He leaned over the edge of the bar. "I want you to create magic," he said in a deep voice he barely recognized.

"You're too old to believe in magic, buster."

If the magic had left her life, he wanted to be the one to restore her faith. Bizarre how quickly she'd gotten to him, but after years of bland women and uninteresting relationships, Logan recognized a gem when he saw one.

"I'm old enough to know what I want, but not too old for you."

"Want to bet?"

"I'm a gambling man." He reached out and tucked a wayward strand of hair behind her ear. The tiny silver pendants hanging from her earlobe were intriguing. A delicate contrast to her sharp tongue and prickly exterior. He lowered his hand, letting his fingers trail down her soft cheek.

She sucked in a startled breath, then coughed into her hand. "Don't read too much into that. I swallowed wrong."

He laughed. "You're hell on a man's ego." Not that he believed her professed disinterest. The rapid flutter of a pulse beating in her neck and the flush of pink that stained her neck and cheeks betrayed her.

"All in a day's work." She smiled.

The flash of white teeth revealed two dimples on either side of her luscious lips. He vowed to taste that smile before the night was out.

"Speak or scram," Catherine said. "What do you want, Mr. Montgomery?"

Time was running out. He glanced into her eyes before leaning close and whispering in her ear.

TO MAKE YOUR DREAMS come true. A thrill spun its way through her veins. At least fifty guests and party favors later, and she still couldn't suppress the tremor of excitement Logan's words brought. Thanks to his husky tone, she knew what he desired, but the sincerity in his eyes made her want to believe he meant more than a cheap fling. Yet after those heart-stealing words, he'd stood, reminded her she had other guests waiting and left, walking through the double doors and into the Montgomery mansion. He'd never looked back.

Her instincts had been right. He'd seen her as an interesting diversion. When she hadn't proved easy, he couldn't be bothered with the chase. She shrugged. No big deal. Hadn't she already backed off herself?

So why was the disappointment so lingering?

She had no doubt Logan Montgomery was a man capable of fulfilling every fantasy she'd imagined and some she probably hadn't. Just the thought of him made her body hum with a sexual awareness she couldn't mistake. Oh, he'd be good and she'd enjoy herself, but this was a man capable of getting inside her soul.

They weren't meant to happen. Not without someone getting hurt. She being the someone who came to mind. One reckless night wasn't worth a sacrifice in self-worth.

And he obviously wasn't interested in pursuing more.

Over the next hour, the clouds darkened and the guests began a slow trickling out of the estate. The budget on this party had enabled her to splurge on everything, including cleanup, and the crew was waiting to take over. The woman they'd hired as manager would supervise the next shift. By this evening, no remnants of the party would remain. Catherine had no reason to stay.

She edged past the few remaining guests and slipped into the wide entryway that led to the coatroom in the foyer. Yellow and white satin wrapped around the circular staircase in the corner and draped like border paper high on the walls. More than once, she cringed as her snea-kered feet squeaked against the freshly waxed marble floor. She entered the closet that was larger than the room she'd shared with her sister growing up and hit the light switch on the wall.

Despite the ominous clouds, the day had started off with potential and the closet was empty of jackets and coats. Catherine's rain slicker, brought more out of foresight than need, stood out in the empty room.

"Gran!"

Catherine turned at the sound of the deep, compelling voice in time to see Logan glance inside the walk-in closet. "Gran!" he called once more. "Is that you?"

"Not unless this party has aged me more than I thought," Catherine said from the back recesses of the room.

He continued his path straight toward her. "Not a chance." His gaze settled on her face, intense and focused. "Beauty and a smart mouth—you're a lethal combination."

She chose to detour around that remark. "I thought you already left." She curled her hand around the soft plastic of her coat, as if a solid grip would keep her safe from her rioting hormones and a sexy man.

"Keeping tabs on me?" he asked with a cocky grin.

"Guest awareness is part of my job."

"Seems to me hiding behind your job is part of your job."

"What's that supposed to mean?" she asked, although she already knew. Logan had obviously seen through her feigned disinterest.

He walked up beside her. His masculine scent tantalized and seduced. A swirling ribbon of desire unfurled in her belly and reached straight to her core.

"I meant every time I try to get close, you scurry behind the job description. Do I scare you, Cat?" His voice lowered a dangerous, seductive octave.

His gaze never wavered. Warm eyes she could drown in locked and held with hers. Did he scare her? More than he could imagine.

"Because that's the last thing I want."

"Then what do you want, Mr. Montgomery?"

He laughed deep in his throat. "Semantics won't keep me at a distance. It's Logan."

"I..."

"Say it."

She licked her dry lips. His gaze followed the movement. "Logan," she murmured more to appease him than to become more intimate.

"Nice. Now as I was saying...I want to erase that cynicism from those beautiful green eyes. I want to make your dreams come true."

His words struck Catherine in her heart. Unfortunately she still didn't believe he saw her as more than an interesting diversion from the more cultured, more beautifully dressed women at the party. Women who would trip over themselves for a chance at landing one of the state's most eligible bachelors.

"You want a good time," she said.

He had the audacity to grin. "That, too."

She wanted to give in to that handsome face and easy smile, which meant she had to get out of here, to her empty apartment where safety and reality would reassert themselves.

"Logan," she said, not wanting to give him further reason to believe he affected her. "I think…"

A loud thud cut her off as the closet door slammed shut behind them. She jumped at the unexpected sound.

"Hold that thought." He touched her lips with one finger. Heat traveled between her mouth and his skin.

A shiver took hold. Desire? Fear? Probably both. Though she liked to flirt, she'd never reacted to a man with such carnal, sensual awareness before.

Before she could think further, he strode to the door and jiggled the door handle. The muted sound of metal hitting the marble floor sounded from outside. He muttered a curse.

"What's wrong?"

"Nothing as long as you aren't claustrophobic." He held the doorknob aloft in his hand. "Looks like the old lady has her own agenda. Not that I mind."

An uncomfortable feeling arose in the pit of her stomach. "What are you saying?" She eyed the doorknob in his hand and shook her head.

He banged on the door with his fist. "Open up, Gran."

"What's your hurry? The company's good and the way things look, you've got plenty of time. I've got to find someone in this house who understands hardware. I think I did serious damage," she called back. The click of heels on the floor sounded as Emma Montgomery walked away.

"She didn't," Catherine said, glaring at the door through narrowed eyes. She wasn't claustrophobic but she disliked the feeling of being trapped. Especially with this man.

"She did." Logan shrugged. "Sorry. She tends to get carried away."

"*She?*"

"You wouldn't be suggesting I set you up?" Disbelief and humor lit his gaze. "I'm interested, not desperate. I can get my woman without Gran's help."

"*Your woman?*" She swallowed a laugh. "That has a Neanderthal sound to it."

He shrugged. "I kind of liked it."

"You would. So how about breaking down the door, Tarzan?"

"If I give it a shot, will you have that drink with me?"

"You wouldn't stoop to using your grandmother, but bribery is okay?"

"Is that a yes?"

She believed he had nothing to do with their current predicament. The eccentric older woman would definitely pull a stunt like this. The only question was why. She certainly couldn't think Catherine was an acceptable choice for her grandson, nor could she believe Logan incapable of getting his own dates.

Speaking of dates, she had a decision to make. The closet, which had seemed so large when she'd first entered, was shrinking by the minute. She couldn't breathe without inhaling the scent of spice and man, an erotic combination that stole her breath and threatened to take her sanity next. One drink in a public place was much safer than hanging out alone with him now.

She glanced at his handsome face and forced a casual shrug. "One drink," she agreed.

She hoped she didn't live to regret those two little words.

CHAPTER THREE

RELIEF AT HER ACCEPTANCE warred with the steady beat of desire pounding inside him. "Should I be flattered that you accepted?" Logan asked. "Or insulted you want out of here so badly?"

"Neither. I accepted because I'm thirsty. Now give it your best shot."

He wouldn't have an inflated ego as long as Catherine was around. Logan was honest enough to admit he wanted her by his side for a long while. Long enough to get to know the cautious woman with the sassy mouth.

He needed time, but time freely given, not under duress. He eyed the door and slugged it as hard as he could with his shoulder. His bad shoulder. Hell, after years of college baseball, both shoulders were bad and this one rebelled against his attempted escape. It rolled in the socket and he groaned in pain.

Catherine was by his side in an instant. "I'm sorry."

"Not your fault," he muttered through gritted teeth. He counted to ten and waited for the pain to subside. Since it often popped out in his sleep, Logan was used to the routine. Slowly the shoulder numbed as the pain eased.

Soft hands reached for his collar. Logan let her slip the jacket off his shoulders. If she wanted to play Florence Nightingale, he'd let her. He wasn't proud that he was taking advantage of her concern. But he doubted he'd have a better chance to catch her with her guard down.

She lowered herself to the floor, her back propped against the wall. "Sit."

Logan sat beside her.

She turned and began working the sore muscles in his arm with her fingertips. The pressure felt so good he groaned in relief. "That feels great. Thanks."

"You're welcome. Now tell me how we ended up like this. What made you think Emma was in here?" Catherine asked.

He leaned his head backward and focused on the rhythmic motion of her fingers pressing through his shirt and into his skin. "The cocktail waitress who said, 'Your grandmother is waiting for you by the coat closet.' Nothing unusual or sinister about that..." Her fingers pushed deep and eased off, caressed and massaged the sore muscle. "Unless you know my grandmother. Mmm. A little deeper."

She complied. Those fingers worked magic and Logan found himself seduced...by her scent, her touch, by her.

"Better?" she asked.

"Much." As close to perfect as he could get without lying naked beside her.

"Someone should come looking for us any minute," she said.

"If you believe that you don't know my grandmother."

"Maybe, but there're plenty of people out there who can handle something as simple as a broken doorknob. The cleaning crew will have no problem fixing the handle."

"Assuming she asks them to or brings their attention to us, which is doubtful." He rolled his head to the side and met her gaze. Desire shimmered in her eyes, just as it pummeled inside of him. "We've got time."

"People might want drinks," she said, but the protest sounded weak.

"Something tells me Emma's handling things as

we speak. Besides, the party was winding down, with the judge holding court, reminding them about the formal breakfast he's holding in the morning."

Logan knew this because he'd spent a ridiculous amount of time assuring his father he would *not* be at the affair, he would *not* meet with future supporters and he most certainly would *not* be at the press announcement next Saturday. He'd have preferred to be in the thick of the party watching Catherine. Instead he'd been beating his head against a brick wall, just as he had too often as a child.

And from the stubborn glint in the judge's eye, he hadn't accepted Logan's words. Too bad. The older man couldn't say he hadn't been warned.

"You always call your father *the judge?*" she asked.

When he called him anything at all, Logan thought. "That's what he is."

"He's also your father."

"Who thinks he rules everyone the same way he does his courtroom."

"And I always thought any father would be preferable to none at all."

So, she had no father in her life. Some more insight. He stored the knowledge, sensing it was an important facet of Catherine's nature, a way to breach her defenses.

"Not always. Don't get me wrong, he's been there for us...as long as we toe the line." That was about to change. Edgar Montgomery might have put up with his son's erratic behavior, as he called it, but only because he believed he'd gain what he wanted in the end. It wouldn't happen this time, which just might cause the ultimate family rift.

"Who's us?" Catherine asked.

"Me and my sister, Grace."

"I have a sister, too. So tell me what it was like growing up here." She made a grandiose gesture with one arm. Obviously *here* meant the Montgomery Estate.

As a general rule, Logan didn't choose to remember his childhood. He'd already divulged more in this one conversation than he had in the past thirty-one years. Along with the memories came an attached fear he would end up as alone as his old man. No matter how many people his father invited into his home, no matter that his wife trailed his every move, the judge was like an island. He allowed people to get near but never close. Not even his children.

For Catherine, a woman who eyed him and his

wealth with obvious suspicion, Logan would dig deep and be honest. "It was lonely," he admitted.

"That's sad." Her hand curled around his and her head eased onto his shoulder.

Stunned, Logan glanced down at their intertwined hands. She'd reached out to him. With the simple truth he'd begun breaching her well-built defenses. Money and status didn't impress her. Honesty did. His respect for Catherine rose.

Pulling herself up to her knees, Catherine faced him, eyes wide, her expression curious. "How could you be lonely with so many people around?" she asked.

"Because no one bothered with us kids... except my grandmother."

Her smile wrapped around his heart. "I like her."

"So do I." And he supposed he owed his grandmother for arranging this get-to-know-you session with Catherine, but he'd still give the old lady a blistering lecture for meddling in his life. Not that it would do any good.

"So tell me how you met my grandmother," he said.

"At a fund-raiser we catered in Boston. She wanted more hor d'oeuvres and snuck into the kitchen to get them."

He burst out laughing. "That sounds like Emma."

Catherine grinned. "I caught her and we started talking. Next thing I knew she'd hired me for the Garden Gala."

He glanced at Catherine and realized he was extremely glad he'd come. "When she's not meddling, my grandmother is one smart lady."

"Because she locked us in here?"

"Because she obviously likes you...and so do I." His gaze locked with hers. Sensual awareness pulsed thick around them.

He cupped his palms around her cheeks, bringing her within kissing distance...and waited. One hint of refusal and he'd let her go. She shook her head and disappointment welled inside him.

He lowered his hands. Her sudden grip on his wrists stopped him. "Don't."

"Don't kiss you or don't pull away? Because I don't play games, Cat. I want you and I know you want me." The sudden hitch in her breathing proved him right.

"What I want and what's good for me are two different things," she whispered.

His mouth brushed hers, deliberately light and excruciatingly slow. He simply tasted her without pushing for more. Her fingers curled into his wrists and a purr escaped her lips. Cat, he thought, recalling his grandmother's use of the endearment, had just earned her nickname.

His restraint was rewarded. She never broke the kiss or the momentum building between them. With this woman only patience would get him what he desired and he believed she was worth it.

Catherine let sensation take over. Logan's lips were firm, his touch gentle. His scent enticed her and his kiss held checked passion and a respect she'd rarely felt from a man. Beneath the gentleness was a longing she felt, too. As a ribbon of desire coiled tight in her belly, the need to be with him overwhelmed her.

Without warning, the clatter of metal startled her and she jumped back, breaking their passionate kiss. One that never should have happened. She burrowed into his white shirt, unwilling to face him just yet.

"Sounds like we're being rescued," he said.

"Sounds like." She forced herself to move. Ignoring the steady pounding of her heart, she stood, refusing to meet his gaze. She'd lost her head, succumbed to desire and Lord only knew what would have happened if they hadn't been rescued.

She started for the door but his light touch on her back stopped her. "You didn't do anything wrong, Cat."

"Who said I did?" she asked defensively. "One kiss isn't such a big deal."

He raised an eyebrow. "One kiss?"

"Unless you can't count."

A slight grin tugged at his lips. "Neither one of us came up for air, so I'll give you that one."

Heat rose to her cheeks. "A real gentleman wouldn't have mentioned that."

"Whoever said I was a gentleman?" He touched the pad of his thumb to her lower lip.

Her entire body shook in reaction. She wrapped her arms around her waist but the effort at self-protection came too late.

"I started it, Cat, and I wish I could say I was sorry. But I won't."

With that statement, he preceded her to the door. She stared at his retreating back and wondered how things had gotten so out of hand. She glanced down at her shaking hands and closed her eyes against the unfulfilled sexual energy still pulsing through her.

She wished lust was all she felt for Logan Montgomery.

Sex was purely physical and easy to leave

behind. Logan wasn't. She'd seen the real man beneath the power suit and playboy charm. She'd caught a glimpse of a lonely little boy growing up in a mausoleum, much like she'd been a lonely child in a tenement apartment. Class differences had vanished. To make matters worse, she'd discovered she liked him. Really liked him. Somewhere between walking into this closet and walking out, *he* had begun to matter. Knowing the inevitable conclusion, the truth chilled her deep inside.

She stared beyond Logan's broad shoulders to the closet door and listened to the sounds of rescue. Seconds later the hinges were off and the entire door had been removed. Without glancing in his direction again, she slid past him and headed for safety. The bright glare of the crystal chandelier hit her hard and she blinked until her eyes adjusted.

Catherine glanced around.

"She wouldn't dare show her face now." Logan's voice sounded from behind her.

It didn't surprise her that he'd read her mind.

"Gran's probably upstairs hiding," he said.

While he turned to thank their rescuers—the cleaning crew, as she had predicted—she pulled herself together. By the time he'd returned to her, she was composed again. Until she caught a glimpse of the makeup stain on the once white collar of his dress shirt.

She cleared her throat. "Well."

He grinned. "Well."

"Goodbye." Feeling ridiculous, she held out her hand.

His warm fingers wrapped around hers. "Not so fast, Cat." Her heart tripped at the shortened name. "You're forgetting something," he said.

"Such as?"

"You owe me a drink and I'd have sworn you were a woman of your word."

Bantering and sparring. Now she was back on familiar ground. Her tension eased. "You didn't get us out of there," she reminded him.

"And I didn't have to. I said I'd give that door a shot and I did." He rubbed his shoulder as a reminder and a blatant attempt to induce guilt.

He was right. Semantics, as he'd called them earlier, had indeed tripped her up. She owed him one drink, but thank the good Lord, it wouldn't be now. At least she'd have a chance to regroup and firmly remind herself that whatever was going on between them was just a fluke.

She glanced down at her work uniform. "I'd rather not go anywhere dressed like this."

"You look good to me." Warm eyes met hers and he extended his hand. "Come with me. You can trust me, Cat."

She stared into those seductive brown eyes. Trust him? She nearly laughed aloud. Hadn't her father said the same thing to her mother the night before he'd walked out for good? If Catherine agreed, would she end up seduced and abandoned the next day? And why was a tiny voice in her head shouting this man was worth the risk?

What was it about good-looking men that made them think they could have the world at their feet with raw sex appeal alone? She eyed him warily. "I can't go anywhere with you. The company van is parked outside—I can't leave it here."

"Bet you it's not. Double or nothing. If I'm wrong, you're free to go. If I'm right, it's drinks *and dinner.*"

She had him this time. "That's a safe enough bet." She patted the outside pockets of her black skirt, then dipped her hand inside. She dangled the van's keys in midair. Five more minutes in his company then she'd be on her way home.

Later she'd deal with the lingering disappointment and sexual humming that still teased her senses. Later, she'd ponder the unfairness of fate, throwing a perfect man into her less than perfect life.

Later. When she was alone.

"Truck or no truck. Time to find out." Logan reached out. He made a grab for the keys, but captured her hand instead.

His fingers wrapped around hers. Warm and trusting. The words came to her in a rush. She shook her head. Sexual awareness had to be short-circuiting her brain. Why else would a woman who'd promised herself she wouldn't fall into a man's trap, be thinking warm and fuzzy thoughts about someone so far out of reach?

She followed him through the house and finally outside. The rain, which had held off for the duration of the party, had released itself at last. Logan wrapped his arm securely around her back as he led her toward the back of the house where the cars were parked. She resented his easy manner, and the bond he'd managed to cement with her in so short a time. Because truck or no truck, a man from Logan Montgomery's world wouldn't want any more from Catherine Luck than a fast tumble and a quick goodbye.

LOGAN TURNED UP THE HEAT in the Jeep. Catherine sat in the seat beside him, her slicker wrapped tightly around her. She stared out the window into the night. The rain had picked up a furious pace, splattering the windshield so hard and fast even the wipers couldn't keep up. Logan was forced to squint to see beyond the steadily falling sheets.

Silence still reigned beside him. He glanced to his right. "Being mad isn't going to help."

"I'm not mad. I'm furious."

"At?"

"Your grandmother, to start. My manager, to finish."

"You heard the staff. Emma assured them you'd taken a tour of the house and she'd promised you a ride home, which I'm providing...just as she'd planned," he muttered under his breath.

What he didn't need right now was a meddling grandmother with her own agenda. Not when this woman trusted so little as it was. He wanted her to take him in, into her confidence...into her bed.

Man, was he in trouble.

"So this detour wasn't on the agenda?" she asked.

"There was no agenda, at least not on my part." And no more games, either. As much as he wanted more time with her, she obviously preferred to go home. Alone. Only slime would force his attentions on an unwilling woman.

He gripped the steering wheel between his fists as he fought increasingly deep puddles of rain on the otherwise slick roads, then slowed the car down even more. "Which way?" he asked.

"You ought to know."

He eased the vehicle over to the shoulder and draped one arm over the wheel. "I'm taking you home, Cat."

Quiet enveloped them once more.

She met his gaze, surprise etched in her features. "Why?"

"You're obviously not here willingly. I thought you'd relax, but I was wrong. I wouldn't want to force you to spend any more time in my company than is absolutely necessary."

She eyed him warily, disbelief emanating from her in waves. "Are you always such a gentleman or is this an act for my benefit?"

He shrugged. "Are you always such a cynic about people's motives?"

"Answering a question with a question," she murmured. "A cop or a lawyer?"

"Lawyer, and we're sharks by reputation, so don't go getting any soft ideas about me." He'd never been a lapdog for any woman before and though he'd probably roll over and beg for her, he wasn't about to admit that aloud. Just the thought had him squirming in his seat.

She laughed. "There are a lot of words I'd use to describe you, Logan Montgomery, and soft isn't one of them."

"Tell me something I don't know," he muttered. With every inhale of her subtle scent, his pants grew tighter.

A fierce blush stained her cheeks. He liked the feminine side that showed her vulnerability. Damn. He had to get the hell out of here. "Like I said earlier, I'm interested, not desperate."

The low murmur of voices in the background reminded him the radio was on and he raised the volume a couple of notches. Just in time, he caught the weather report warning of flash floods and dangerous wind and lightning, especially near the ocean.

He lowered the radio. "Directions?" he prodded, wanting to get her home safely.

The crisp ping of rain hitting the windshield sounded around them, proof that, for once, the weatherman was on target. If they didn't get going soon, the driving would be even more treacherous than it already was. Even if he got her home, wherever home was, he wouldn't make it back again.

He glanced at her wary expression and doubted she would offer her hospitality. Not that he blamed her. After his grandmother's shenanigans, Catherine probably wouldn't even lend the use of her floor as a makeshift bed. He'd be forced to take a motel room he preferred not to waste his money on.

Living off his salary as a public defender hadn't been a problem until he'd decided to buy and renovate his new home—make that his old home that needed extensive work. The solitude and view of the ocean made living on a shoestring budget worthwhile. No way he'd sacrifice his independence by living off the trust set up for him as a child.

He glanced at his passenger. "I'd like to get you home dry and in one piece, Cat."

She sighed, but the beginnings of an unexpected smile fought its way to her lips. "What's so amusing?" he asked.

"You make it extremely hard to dislike you."

He reached out and stroked his hand down her soft cheek. "That wasn't my point...but I can't say I'm disappointed."

Catherine curled her knees onto the seat as she

studied the man beside her. She'd thought him charming, but that was an understatement. Appealing might be a better word. He knew how to turn a situation to his advantage without making her feel as if she'd been manipulated. Just when she'd gathered her defenses against his polished charm and good looks, he struck with deadly accuracy. He acted out of respect for her well-being and concern for her wishes. She still wasn't sure she could trust him. Worse, she wasn't sure she could trust herself.

He eased the car back onto the wet road. "So where do you live anyway?" he asked.

"Downtown Boston."

He groaned. "That's nearly an hour from here."

"That's why I'd planned on staying at my sister's tonight."

The car ahead of them made a sudden stop and he swerved to avoid hitting the vehicle. The Jeep hydroplaned across the slick roads, nearly sending them into a skid. She gripped the dashboard with both hands. He swore under his breath, then maneuvered them back with more skill than she would have possessed. "You okay?" he asked.

"Fine." She let out a shaky breath. No way

they'd make it as far as her sister's house—a good half hour from here, Catherine thought. Not in this weather.

She bit the inside of her cheek. Why was fate conspiring to keep her with a man who was so obviously wrong for her? Though he'd breached her reserve, she had lived long enough to understand there were still social classes that couldn't be crossed into.

"My place is ten minutes from here. How far is your sister's?" Logan asked.

"Too far," she muttered.

He raised an eyebrow while keeping his gaze on the road. "My place it is."

Catherine remained silent. There wasn't much to say. She'd take a look at his expensive house and valuable accessories and know for certain they had nothing in common besides lust. He'd realize the same thing.

"Where are we headed, exactly?" she asked.

"A small cottage on the beach. Another couple of minutes tops."

"Small cottage?" She laughed aloud. "I can't wait to see it." Catherine eased back in her seat, anticipation warring with apprehension. As much as she couldn't help but look forward to the few more hours they'd share, she knew one glimpse at his *small* cottage would cement the truth in her mind. They didn't stand a chance.

They made the rest of the trip in silence. Catherine didn't want to risk another near accident by distracting Logan and he seemed engrossed in his driving. He pulled onto a private driveway that ran parallel to the beach. At the far end stood a true beachfront home.

A Cape-styled cottage, it boasted typical New England charm with a single peak and ample windows, but was smaller than Catherine had imagined. Much smaller, especially when compared with the Montgomery Estate.

He slowed the car to a stop and shut the ignition. Without the sound of the engine, the rain pelted loud and clear against the windshield.

"It's humble but it's home."

A traditional cape home right on the ocean, it was cozy and comforting, tempting and alluring. Like the man himself. She barely knew him but she sensed she was in deep. She let out a long breath. *Catherine Ann, you are probably in big trouble.*

"Like it?" he asked.

"It's incredible," she murmured.

Logan glanced up toward the black sky and torrential sheets of rain. "I hope you mean it..." His potent gaze strayed to hers. "Because if the rain keeps up at this pace, we could be stranded. Beach roads flood pretty quickly around here."

"I could think of worse things," she said, her voice unusually thick. She bit down on her lower lip. Temptation to turn the radio back on warred with the desire to close off the outside world for as long as she could. Even if she did hear the weather report again, nothing would change whether they'd be stranded together or not.

Fate had just handed over her heart's secret desire. A night alone with Logan Montgomery, if she was brave enough to take it. She shut her eyes and listened to the heavy sound of the rain beating against the windshield, in cadence to the rapid pounding of her heart. In time to the building crescendo of need inside her.

A crash of thunder startled her and she jumped in her seat. From their parked position, far from the house, Catherine had a good view of the ocean and the waves crashing fast and furious against the shore. Having grown up in the city and with little time for trips to the beach, the notion of the undertow had always both frightened and intrigued her.

The angry waves rolled forward onto the sand, then retreated without warning. Sort of like the ebb and flow of desire between a man and a woman, she thought and a violent tremor shook her body.

He placed a warm hand on her shoulder. "You okay?" he asked.

He obviously meant to reassure, but his touch had the opposite effect and sent her senses soaring. She needed to get out of this car and make a grab for sanity. "Can you pull a little closer?" she asked.

"I wish." He slung one arm over the back of her seat. "Here we're on paved road. Beyond us is mud."

She followed his gaze and stared out the window. Although visibility was awful, she realized he was right. "Okay. I'm a good sport. They say rainwater's good for the skin and fresh air is even better for the soul. And besides, I'm wearing sneakers."

He grinned. "That's the spirit. I'd offer to race you but the terrain can get pretty slippery when wet." He got out of the car and came around her side to help her out. She held on to his hand. "Ready?" he asked.

Another crash of thunder broke the monotony of the rain, and was followed by an unexpected flash of lightning. Her heart leaped in her chest. "I'm ready."

The run for the house wasn't easy. She sloshed through puddles, slipped on mud and held on to Logan's hand, nearly taking him down more than once. The rain poured on them hard and left them soaked. But by the time they reached the house, Catherine wasn't miserable, she was laughing.

Just before Logan put the key into the lock, he paused and met her gaze. An unexpected, electrical connection sizzled between them and, in that moment, Catherine knew.

Trouble waited just inside the door.

CHAPTER FOUR

THE STORM RAGING OUTSIDE was nothing compared to the one wreaking havoc inside of Catherine. She stepped inside the house and found both a haven from the rain and a look into Logan's soul.

"Hang on a second. I'll be right back." He left Catherine standing in a warm and cozy den.

The room, like the house, offered a reflection of the man. The scarred, wood-paneled walls were as masculine as Logan, as welcoming as his personality. A beat-up brown leather sofa and old wood furniture lent a comfortable charm to the rustic interior of the house.

Although she lived in a one-bedroom apartment, she and Logan obviously shared a deep longing for hearth and home because the warm brown tones and coziness in many ways matched her personal taste and style. In fact, any one of her animal-print area rugs, throw blankets or pillows would add spice and a bit of life to the already near perfect atmosphere.

No formal entryways, marble floors or crystal chandeliers in this home. And judging from the relaxed atmosphere, that's what it was—a home lacking in the luxury known and loved by the rest of the Montgomery clan. What kind of statement did Logan think he was making living in a place like this? Was he being deliberately contrary toward his family or did he genuinely love the smell of the ocean and the cabin's earthy appeal?

She couldn't help but wonder what his family thought of his place of residence. She'd bet very few family dinners were held here and the thought made her sad. Though she hadn't had a traditional upbringing, either, she'd sensed Logan longed for one the same way she did.

"Towel?" He reappeared with two in his hand.

"Thanks." He tossed one her way. Catherine peeled off her slicker and glanced around for a closet or someplace to put her jacket.

"I'll take it," he said, then hung her coat on a wooden coat stand already laden with more jackets than it could probably handle. "Easier than tossing them on the couch," he said with a grin.

A smile tugged at her lips. "You're a man. I'm amazed they make it as far as a coat hook."

"You shouldn't stereotype someone before you get to know them," he said, warm humor in his voice. "They might just end up surprising you."

"Are you saying you're not a typical male?"

"I'm saying you're about to find out."

Was he throwing out a challenge, waiting for her to back away? If so, he'd be disappointed. She'd come this far and Catherine intended to see things through, wherever they led. She wasn't sure when her decision had been made but a rush of excitement flooded her veins.

She licked her dry lips. "So you're a neat man. I'm impressed," she murmured.

"I should hope so," he said in a deep voice. "Besides, some things just weren't permitted while I was growing up. Leaving a trail of clothes behind me was one of them." He shrugged. "Old habits die hard, I guess."

"Don't tell me you didn't have help to pick up after you."

"Of course I did. But one hit upside the head by Emma and I was cured of that nasty habit for life."

The vision was absurd, yet Catherine believed him. Emma spoke her mind and got what she wanted. A tremor rippled through her as she realized the implications—Logan had been raised by his grandmother. He, too, spoke his mind. And she sensed he also got what he wanted.

"Besides," he said, "Emma was right." The light and laughter in his eyes spoke of his love for his grandmother and Catherine's respect for Logan grew. How could she not like a man with the ability to laugh at himself? A man who humored an old woman and wasn't ashamed to let his love for her shine through.

"The help had their hands full catering to my parents. They didn't need two spoiled kids added to the mix."

"So you're also a man who isn't afraid to admit when he's wrong."

He raised an eyebrow. "I told you I'm unique," he said with a grin. "And about me being wrong? It doesn't happen all that often."

"Arrogance is a typical masculine quality," she warned him.

"I said I was unique but I never denied being male."

As if she needed any reminders of his potent masculinity. Catherine gripped the soft towel tightly in her hand. "Emma kept you grounded, didn't she?" she asked, deliberately changing the subject.

"You bet she did," he said, drying his hair as he spoke. When he finished, he draped the towel over his broad shoulders.

That simple gesture was all it took to bring his masculinity and her reaction to it flooding back. His tie hung loosely around his neck and he'd opened the restricting collar of his shirt. His hair, damp and disheveled, created a rumpled appearance, making him look even sexier than he had earlier. Catherine hadn't thought he could get any better. She'd been wrong.

Her gaze locked with his. Those dark, compelling eyes lingered on her in what felt like a heated caress. Yet he hadn't lifted a hand, hadn't touched any part of her body. It was only a matter of time.

Silence grew thick around them, but she couldn't bring herself to glance away. Just looking at Logan caused a fluttering sensation in her stomach and a delicious throbbing need between her legs. He stepped closer and her pulse kicked into high gear. Her heart rate soared. His steady gaze never veered from hers as he eased the towel out of her shaking hands and walked around until he stood behind her.

She could no longer see him but she couldn't mistake his presence. His body heat melded with hers and his breathing became a sexy, seductive hum in her ears. Without warning, the warm towel draped over her head and his strong hands began a rhythmic motion as he dried her hair and kneaded her scalp. Unable to help herself, she closed her eyes and leaned back into the hard planes of his chest.

No sooner did she shut her eyes, than her other senses took over. The sound of the rain beating against the house in torrential windswept sheets sounded loud in her ears. Or was it her heartbeat she heard so strongly? The need she felt was stronger than anything she'd experienced before.

Sensation took over. The light tugging at her scalp found an answering pull in other areas of her body. His arms rested on her shoulders, his hands worked at her hair—and her breasts grew heavy as an erotic pull began deep in her stomach, sending shock waves deeper, lower...

A purring noise startled her out of her sensual daydream and Catherine was shocked to realize the sound had come from her. An unexpected crack of thunder followed, and she jumped back, out of his reach.

Her heart beat fast and furious. It wasn't fear of the storm driving her now but unbounded desire. She shook with unrestrained need. A need so strong it both consumed and unnerved her. "I can take it from here," she said.

"Suit yourself, but first…" He reached for the end of the towel. His trembling hands and ragged breathing gave her a sense of comfort. The desire wasn't one-sided. He wiped down her face with gentle pats that shouldn't have felt sexy but did.

"Mascara," he explained, revealing black stains on the pale towel.

"Oh." She bit down on her lower lip. "Thank you."

"My pleasure." As his darkened gaze met hers, Catherine knew exactly what he meant.

"Why don't you get out of those wet clothes?" he asked.

She tipped her head to one side. "Don't you think you're rushing things?"

He laughed. "I didn't say *I'd* get you out of those clothes, though I could be persuaded."

"You're bad," she said, unable to hold back the laughter.

"Care to find out just how bad?" Before she could formulate a comeback, he reached for her hand. "Come on. Those clothes are wet and you must be freezing. I'm sure I can scrounge up a pair of drawstring sweats for you."

"I'd appreciate that."

Five minutes later, she found herself alone in a small bathroom with an old-fashioned tub and an even older shower. Dry clothes sat on the vanity. Logan's clothes.

She picked up the soft sweats and held them to her face. She breathed in deeply. The clothes smelled clean and fresh but they also held the slightest hint of Logan's scent. Catherine didn't know if the masculine scent was real or existed only in her imagination but it didn't matter. The sensual aura of spicy aftershave affected her either way. A tremor shook her that had nothing to do with being wet or cold, but had everything to do with Logan Montgomery.

She was in his home, wearing his clothes, and allowing herself to be emotionally seduced—as much by his contradictions as by the man himself. Nothing was as it should be.

Logan wasn't as artificial and stuffy as the Montgomery name and tradition dictated he ought to be. He shouldn't be interested in a woman outside his world, yet after seeing his home, Catherine wasn't sure *what* world Logan inhabited. Which meant she wasn't sure what kind of allure she held for him. At this point, she could almost believe in impossible dreams.

Dangerous, she thought. But so very tempting.

She flipped on the shower faucets. Time for grounding herself. He might live here, but given the luxury with which he'd grown up, and the people with whom he was raised, he had to have an ulterior motive, one that might just include her as well. And even if he was sincere, the novelty of a woman like Catherine would wear off fast for a man with the name Montgomery.

THE SHOWER WATER SOUNDED unnaturally loud in the small cottage. Logan should have been surprised he could distinguish the shower noise over the pounding wind and rain outside. He wasn't. Not when Catherine was in the next room, water running down her supple curves. He braced his hands against the kitchen counter, lowered his head and let out a slow groan.

He'd had his hands in her hair and she'd sighed like he was inside her body. She was so responsive to the simplest touch, it was enough to drive him mad. She was also losing her inhibitions around him. But he had to take it slow to avoid losing any headway he'd made.

The shower water stopped, leaving him in silence. He had the whole night ahead of him to win her trust... and maybe more. A lot more, he hoped. But her trust was more important than getting her into bed. And that in itself was a warning he knew he'd better heed.

"Hi," Catherine said.

"Hi, yourself." Logan turned from where he'd been scrounging through the refrigerator and his breath caught in his throat.

Blond hair that had been tied up in a knot above her head now curled in damp strands around her makeup-free face. Her skin was nearly flawless, fair and translucent, touched by an endearing pink flush on her cheeks. The curves that had been so obvious earlier were now hidden by soft cotton. She'd had to roll the sleeves more than a few times and the elastic bottom of each pant leg. The effect was a startling blend of sweetness and vulnerability, two words he hadn't associated with this woman before now.

He'd seen her dressed for work. He'd seen her wet and disheveled from a run in the rain. And though he'd found her more desirable with each transformation, this one left him speechless. Because the soft and approachable woman wearing *his* clothes, standing in *his* kitchen touched his heart.

"Can I help?" she asked. "I know my way around the kitchen."

"Which makes you a typical woman?" he asked, falling back on their earlier banter.

She clucked her tongue. "I'm anything but typical." She sniffed, pretending to be offended.

He laughed. "Believe me, I knew that or you wouldn't be here right now. You're special, Cat."

A blush rose to her cheeks. "Cut that out before you embarrass me."

"A woman who doesn't go looking for compliments. Now that's unusual."

She shrugged. "Sounds to me like you know the wrong women."

"But at least I've found the right one. Now, I know catering is your business, but I didn't realize you had hands-on experience behind the scenes as well."

She pushed up the rolled sleeves only to have them fall down again. "You'd be surprised. I have years of restaurant experience behind me and I'm not talking just washing dishes."

"We have all night for you to fill me in. Why don't you sit and let me handle things?"

Catherine shrugged and headed for a chair by the kitchen table. "A man who can cook! Another blow to the stereotypical male."

"I hate to disillusion you." He reached inside the refrigerator and came out with a covered casserole dish. "But I have no choice. This lasagna is the best Emma's cook can prepare," he said with a laugh.

Catherine laid a hand over her heart. "You're destroying my fantasies."

He shook his head, then walked over to where she sat. Bracing his hands on the arms of her chair, he leaned so close he could taste her—if he chose. Sensing she was not yet ready, he refrained. "I'm not going to destroy your fantasies, Cat. I'm going to make them come true."

Before she could blink, he rose and strode back to the lasagna on the counter. Distance gave him a chance to cool off before he acted against common sense and blew things for sure.

"At least you have Emma. She makes sure you don't starve," Catherine said.

"Embarrassing to admit, but yes. What do you know about the public defender's office hours?" he asked as he took the foil wrap off the casserole dish.

"Not much."

"Then let me fill you in." Details of his own life might encourage her to reveal facts of her own and Logan wanted to know everything about her. "I'm on call three nights a week and one weekend a month for courtroom duty. When

I'm not there or at the office, I'm bringing home files to work on. There's not much free time for cooking and I'm enough of a man to admit I like to eat." He shrugged. "I may turn my back on plenty of Montgomery family rituals, but I'd never turn away a free meal," he said with a grin.

"I'll remember that." An intriguing gleam lit her green eyes. She rested her chin on her hands. "It's nice you have her to look out for you."

"You're right." He placed the casserole inside the microwave, his only concession to new appliances when he'd moved in.

"So with hours like that, tell me why you'd choose the public defender's office."

"As opposed to some high-powered law firm in Boston?" he asked, the edge in his voice unmistakable. "One that helps institutions not people? One the judge handpicked based on reputation?" His father would have pulled whatever strings possible to settle Logan into a position of power and prestige, regardless of what Logan wanted out of his life and career. As a result, Logan couldn't hide the disgust he felt for the direction the judge wanted his son's career to take.

At his biting tone, she stiffened in her chair. "I meant as opposed to single practice, or in-house counsel. Or maybe setting up a stand on the street and giving advice out for a quarter. What is it with you? I hit a nerve, so you strike back?"

"In a word, yes." He cursed his inability to cover his frustration with his father and hated that he'd taken it out on her. "But it wasn't right and I'm sorry."

Her expression softened. "You really are a man who can admit when he's wrong. Very unique," she murmured. "And I didn't mean to tread on sensitive ground. Or to insult you. I'm just surprised at the road you've taken."

"Tell me something. What's the real reason my career choice surprises you? Is it because you can't picture me helping the downtrodden or because anyone with the name Montgomery should be a self-serving snob?" He joined her at the wooden table.

Reaching his hand across the Formica top, he opened his fist palm upward in a silent signal for her to place her hand in his. "I'm not criticizing you, Cat, any more than I would judge you based on appearances."

"And you'd appreciate it if I did the same for you." A whisper of a smile touched her lips. "I think you caught me revealing my bias against the upper class."

"Instead of judging me based on what you know about me."

She glanced at his hand extended in invitation. "But I hardly know you."

"Oh, I think you do." He kept his palm faceup and never let his gaze stray from hers. "Trust *me*, Cat."

She hesitated. To Logan those seconds felt like an eternity, until finally she joined her hand with his.

Soft and smooth, her skin felt like silk to his touch. Enjoying the feel of her, he brushed his thumb over the pulse point in her wrist. She merely stared, her eyes glittering like emeralds as she waited for his next move.

"So tell me about yourself."

She blinked, obviously startled by his question. But Logan had his reasons. He didn't plan on wasting one minute of the time he had her to himself. "Why don't you start with your family?" he asked when she didn't answer right away.

She shrugged. "Not much to tell. Like you, I have a sister. We share the running of the business but right now she's pregnant and on bed rest. She's married to an arrogant cop." Her grin was at odds with her choice of words. Obviously she didn't dislike the man as much as she proclaimed.

"Anyone else?"

She shook her head. "My mom died years ago and Dad walked out when we were young. I don't even remember him. And then I had an aunt and uncle but they…" Catherine paused and Logan sensed she was debating revealing her family history. "They died last year."

He didn't blame her for keeping quiet. Emma's revelations about her uncle probably wasn't something Catherine considered first-date conversation. He wasn't bothered. She'd have plenty of time to learn to trust and confide in him.

"That's a lot of loss," he said.

She shrugged. "It's life."

He wondered how much of that cavalier attitude had been shaped by necessity, how much by being so alone. "Is your sister older or younger?"

"Kayla's younger by only ten months but she's the more centered sister."

He narrowed his eyes. Logan didn't like the hint of self-criticism in her words. "Something tells me you're not giving yourself enough credit."

She cocked her head to the side. "I think I know myself better than you."

He glanced down at the hand he still held in

his. He turned her hand palm upward and traced the fine lines in her skin. A subtle tremor shot through her and her body visibly shook in reaction.

He smiled, pleased. "Maybe so. But I'd like to know you as well as you know yourself. And I just watched you cater an entire party under stressful conditions—successfully, I might add. So putting yourself second to your sister doesn't cut it for me."

"There's a difference between putting yourself second and knowing your strengths and weaknesses. The only way to be successful in life is to know yourself. Inside and out."

"You impress me, Ms. Luck."

She grinned. "Thank you, Mr. Montgomery."

"It's Logan, remember?"

Catherine remembered. Every minute inside that closet was etched in her memory. She licked her dry lips and his gaze followed the unconscious movement.

"Now care to tell me why a party that had the guests raving had you so uptight?"

Her emotions warred inside her. Pleasure that Logan approved of her job performance fought with wariness of his motives for complimenting her. Alone in his house, seduction couldn't be far from his mind. Heaven knows it wasn't far from hers.

He held her hand in a gentle yet strong and self-assured grip. That light touch alone sent her senses soaring. "I cater parties for a living. This one wasn't any more stressful than m-most." As the lie rolled off her tongue, she felt herself begin to stammer.

As a master of the flippant comeback, Catherine found herself at a sudden loss. She'd never been so flustered before, which said much about her growing feelings for Logan. She didn't like lying to him and yet she couldn't bring herself to admit his father's disapproval had tainted an otherwise successful day. Or that she feared he'd blacklist her company instead of recommending it.

"I don't believe you."

A grin caught hold despite her negative thoughts. "I didn't think you would. But I do appreciate your faith in me—I mean, my abilities."

"Easy to have faith when it's been earned."

The telephone rang then, saving her from having to answer. Logan shot her a regretful look before easing his hand from hers. She felt the glide of his rougher skin as it slid away and she most definitely felt the loss.

He walked across the room, a confidence to his stride that would be hard to miss. Catherine sighed. He was a man with presence. A man with enough sex appeal to make a woman feel alive. Cherished.

He picked up the phone on the third ring. "Hello." He hesitated a beat. "Yes, Gran, I got Cat home fine." He paused. "Whose home?" Logan glanced at her and winked. "Whose home do you think?" he asked. "Don't worry, okay? She's home safe and sound. We both are."

Catherine listened as Logan humored his grandmother, while protecting her own privacy. She appreciated his discretion and almost envied him the older woman's strength and love. She'd never had someone that stable to rely on, unless she counted her sister. Catherine smiled. At least she could always count on Kayla.

"No, I don't want to talk to the judge." Logan's voice drew her back to the present. "Gran? I said no. Tell him... Hello, Dad."

Catherine stifled a groan. The last thing she needed was a reminder of their differences, not when they seemed so minimal when they were together. His father, the infamous Judge Montgomery, managed to make her feel insecure by his very presence in Logan's life.

"No. No breakfast tomorrow. I won't be hungry."

Catherine had to laugh.

"Running for mayor? I plan to be too worn out to run anywhere tomorrow. I have to go... No. I'm hanging up now. Bye." Logan slammed the handset back onto the wall before his father could possibly respond.

He met Catherine's gaze with an amused one of his own. "Emma's golden rule. If you tell someone you're hanging up, they haven't been hung up on," he explained with a grin.

"I suppose I should remember that."

"Might come in handy sometime," he agreed.

"Your grandmother is a piece of work." Still Catherine couldn't help but like the older woman. The more she learned about Logan's childhood and his relationship with Emma, the more her respect for the woman grew. If Logan was a decent man, and Catherine sensed the answer was a resounding yes, then Emma deserved the credit.

Logan nodded. "She likes to think so. Keeps her young and healthy in here." He tapped his head. "And keeps me on my toes."

Catherine agreed with him there. "She locked us in the coat closet. I'd say you have your hands full staying one step ahead of her."

"Sometimes it's not worth the effort. After all, she got the upper hand today and look where it got us." His heavy-lidded gaze strayed to hers. His eyes held warmth and a signal she couldn't possibly mistake.

"And where would that be?"

"Alone, together, if you want us to be."

So the next move was up to her. She shouldn't be surprised. Logan had been a gentleman from the first moment they'd met. He wouldn't stop just because he had her alone in his home. If anything, in the past couple of hours he'd become more sensitive to her feelings.

He offered Catherine many things she'd never received before—respect, admiration and a sense of acceptance. That he desired her went without saying. That he'd let her control what, if anything, happened between them put him in a class by himself.

She chuckled. He already was.

"The choice is yours, Cat." His husky voice was deep and warm, comforting like a friend and se-ductive like a lover's caress. She shivered at the thought.

Silence stretched between them until she couldn't stand the strain. There was nothing holding Cathe-rine back from being with Logan except...

The loud beeps of the microwave announced that dinner was ready—and saved Catherine from herself, at least for now.

CHAPTER FIVE

CATHERINE SAT ON THE COUCH browsing through a magazine. The backside of the den had many windows, offering a magnificent view of the ocean. The sound of the steady rain, along with that of the waves crashing onto shore and rolling back again, sent her senses reeling. She'd always loved the rain and the heavy rhythmic sounds.

She closed her eyes and the sounds became even stronger, so did the pulsing within her. Her desire for Logan, evidenced by the insistent longing between her legs couldn't be denied. She squeezed her legs tight and rolling waves of pleasure crested and ebbed, just like the water on the beach. Just like the pleasure she'd find by making love with Logan, his body inside hers, finding the perfect rhythm, rocking together until the crescendo became the ultimate peak of pleasure.

She forced her eyes open and realized she was

shaking with need. A glance back toward the kitchen told her she was still alone. Considering she could bring herself to the edge with daydreams of Logan, Catherine knew she was in trouble. Better to concentrate on dessert, she thought. The edible kind.

Logan had promised to cook his favorite dessert, one that was handmade, not prepared by Emma's chef. But he wouldn't let her watch. By the time she'd pored over every back issue of *Entertainment Weekly*, Emma's favorite magazine, that she could find, Catherine had cooled her body off to a respectable level. But she couldn't stand to be alone with her erotic thoughts anymore.

She tiptoed to the kitchen and peeked inside. The room itself was old, the appliances dated, but the dark wood cabinets had appeal and potential, and she was sure they'd be dynamite once they were refinished as Logan planned. He puttered around the kitchen, muttering aloud. She couldn't catch a glimpse of what he was making and to walk inside would be to risk getting caught.

She took one silent step backward, when an unexpected flash of lightning flickered from the windows behind her, followed by the loudest crash of thunder yet.

Startled, Catherine shrieked and Logan whirled around.

He raised an amused eyebrow. "Don't tell me. You're afraid of the storm and came seeking comfort."

She rolled her eyes, knowing she'd been had. "I give. You caught me red-handed."

"You're a bad girl, Cat. Now turn around and wait in the den. I'll be out in a second. Surely you can wait that long?" he asked with a charming grin.

"I'll manage somehow." She headed back to the other room. "Me, banished from the kitchen. Who'd ever believe it," she muttered.

The telephone rang and Logan called out from the kitchen, "Can you grab that?"

She picked up the phone beside the couch. "Logan Montgomery's cabin on the ocean. Who may I say is calling?"

Emma's distinctive chuckle was her immediate response. *"She's home safe and sound,"* Emma said in a baritone imitation of Logan. "Did he really think I'd buy that line? His father may fall for that dry wit, but no way can he get anything past me. Women are much smarter than men. You remember that, dear."

"Yes, ma'am." Catherine laughed, surprisingly

not the least bit embarrassed to be caught by Emma at Logan's place. "I *am* home safe and sound. It's just not my home."

"Minor point. At least you're dry and out of the storm."

"I'm out of the closet, too, no thanks to you."

Emma made a *tsking* sound. "They don't make those doorknobs like they used to. The sucker just came off in my hand. Imagine that."

"Who's on the phone?" Logan walked into the den, a tray in his hands.

"Your grandmother. We were just discussing the closet incident."

"Keep her on the phone. I have a few words to say on that subject, too," he said.

"Emma? Logan would like to speak to..."

"My weekly card game awaits. I have to run."

"But..."

"I'm hanging up now," Emma said before doing just that.

Catherine stared at the receiver in hand, then glanced up at Logan. "Weekly card game?" she asked. "On the same night as a huge party? Doesn't seem plausible to me."

He placed the tray down by the fireplace. "Solitaire," he explained, and rolled his eyes, laughter dancing in his gaze.

"Oh, brother."

"She's a master at avoidance. Ready for dessert?"

"Ready to sample your culinary talents, you mean?" Catherine sat on her knees as Logan moved the tray to a low table by the couch. She leaned forward and glanced at two glass holders containing what looked like...she leaned closer and sniffed. "Chocolate pudding?" she asked.

"Only *the* best chocolate pudding you've ever had." He dipped a spoon into the creamy dessert and held it out for her to taste.

She opened her mouth wide and Logan placed the spoon inside, all the while his gaze never leaving her lips. Catherine's body heated up all over again. She closed her eyes and swallowed the delicious chocolate confection.

"Yum." She opened her eyes to find Logan still staring. His intensity had her shaking with need and anticipation all over again. She licked her lips, tasting the chocolate again. "Jell-O brand?" she asked, searching for ordinary conversation to calm down her body.

He placed a hand over his heart. "Would I serve such an extraordinary woman such an ordinary dessert? You wound me. Hell, you don't give me enough credit, Cat." He hesitated only an instant before caving. "It's Jell-O," he muttered.

She grinned. "It's my absolute favorite dessert, too. When I was in culinary school they used to tease me all the time that for someone with the ability to whip up the most intricate desserts, I had the taste of a peasant."

"Did you just say culinary school?"

She grinned. "Yup."

"I made Jell-O instant pudding for an expert?"

"Yup. But don't worry. I know this was last minute and nothing's easier than milk and mix from a box. I don't expect anything like tiramisu until the second date, at least." She glanced over. "What's the matter? You look green."

"Wounded is more like it. A man's ego is a fragile thing."

She laughed and finished off her pudding in a couple of healthy spoonfuls. "That was *the* best pudding I've ever eaten. I don't think even choco-late mousse can compare." Giggling, Catherine continued. "Your talent in the kitchen is unsur-passed. I—"

He cut her off by swiping a finger across her lips. His touch was electric and her laughter came to a sudden halt.

"You had pudding on your lips. See?" He held up his chocolate-smeared finger.

She nodded, unable to speak, somehow knowing what would happen next. He met her gaze. His brown eyes, the color of the rich pudding, glittered with desire.

"Want to finish it off?" he asked.

Drawn by his compelling gaze, lured by the depth of his voice and the sizzling desire burning between them, Catherine leaned forward. She never wavered, never let her gaze veer from his, as her lips closed over his finger. Chocolate mixed with the salty taste of his skin as she licked and finished off the last of the pudding.

Long after he should have pulled back, his finger remained, and he traced the outline of her lips. "Better than licking the bowl, huh?" he asked.

"Much," she whispered. He'd removed his hand, but she didn't know if she could say any more. Her lips tingled. So did her body. Even her breasts had pulled into tight peaks that longed for Logan's touch.

She wondered if he could read her mind. If he knew how much she wanted him. If he reached out and cupped her breasts in his hand, she wouldn't mind. Right now she'd welcome any touch he offered, anything to soothe the raging need he'd inspired.

She drew a deep breath. "I really should clean up."

"Running away?" he asked, his breathing as ragged as hers.

"Taking a time-out."

He leaned back, resting against his palms. His gaze never wavered. "Just don't take too long."

CATHERINE ENTERED the family room in time to see Logan wadding up balls of newspaper and feeding them into the fireplace. He'd begun a small fire that was rapidly growing. He fed the flames, much the same way the desire raged between them, begging to be fueled with more than just a caress.

Since he'd cooked, the least she could do was clean up. He hadn't liked it, but she'd insisted because it was the polite thing to do and because she'd needed distance from his magnetic appeal. The mindless work of washing dishes should have helped. After all, she understood the grind of dishwashing better than most.

When she was sixteen, she'd begun hanging out with the wrong crowd—an excuse to stay out of the empty, lonely apartment where they lived.

Kayla did the same, but she'd been smart enough even then to choose the public library as a place to hide. Catherine hadn't been as bright and, as a result, one night she and her so-called friends had gone out for dinner, to a restaurant not one of them could afford. Although Catherine hadn't known it at the time the other kids had thought it would be a blast to sneak out without paying the bill. Thanks to Kayla's well-meaning concern, that night Catherine was minus her wallet, since her sister thought it would keep her from going out and hanging with the wrong crowd. Kayla had been wrong.

Catherine had gone anyway, then hesitated a second too long when it was time to get out of there. She'd been the only one with any sense of guilt—and the only one who'd gotten caught. A local cop had brought her home and she'd spent the rest of her summer washing dishes in the restaurant kitchen. She was lucky she hadn't spent the night in jail.

She'd always be grateful to the restaurant owner. Not because he hadn't pressed charges but because he'd turned her life around. He was responsible for her interest in cooking and catering. He'd given her a job and the safe, welcoming haven she'd never had.

Catherine smiled at the memory. She hadn't thought of Otto and his wife in years. Obviously Logan's closeness with his grandmother brought out the better memories of her childhood. They weren't all bad as she sometimes thought. Even dishwashing had its good points. But apparently the mindless work hadn't given her the distance or perspective she'd hoped for tonight, because her body was still wound tight.

She glanced at Logan in silence. He'd showered and changed while she was in the kitchen. The intriguing muscles in his back rippled beneath a soft cotton T-shirt and his broad shoulders flexed with each reach for the newspaper by his side.

She wanted to feel the ripple of those muscles beneath her fingertips, to pull his shirt off and plaster her body against his and let the heat of his skin brand her as his own. Catherine bit down on her lower lip. She was in deep.

The thought gave her little comfort. "I'm back."

He glanced over his shoulder. "I'll be done in a second."

She walked toward the welcoming fire and took a seat on the floor in front of the couch. "Fire in the spring?" she asked.

"Why not? If you want something, why not make it happen?"

"Next thing I know you'll tell me you can make it snow in summer," she mused.

He laughed. "You don't make anything easy, do you?"

"Would it be worth it if I did?"

"Touché." He groaned and shifted his attention back to the fire. "This is just one of the perks of living by the water." He stood, hands on his thighs as he rose to his feet. "Since it's always cooler here you can take advantage of the nighttime chill…or the daytime heat."

His darkened gaze met hers. There was no chill in the air now and the fire had nothing to do with the heat arcing between them.

"Music?" he asked.

She nodded. "Something quiet. Mellow." Without thought she reached for her head and began a steady massaging of her temples.

"Something wrong?" He came up beside her.

"Just a slight headache. Postparty letdown," she explained. "I get one after every big event."

"Release of the stress you claimed you didn't have," he said with a grin.

"Exactly."

He walked over to a CD player, and after

removing the one inside and replacing it with another, he hit play. Mellow jazz music surrounded them. Logan came up behind her and eased himself onto the floor.

"Is the music okay?" he asked.

"It's wonderful." The low strains of the music were soothing. Between the party today and the sexual tension throbbing inside her, she was wound tight. His choice in music was the perfect antidote for her stress and she felt the tension in her shoulders and back begin to ease.

"And the head? How's that?"

"Hurts," she admitted.

He settled himself back against the couch and motioned for her to sit between his legs. "Lucky for you I have just the cure." His darkened gaze met hers. "Come here, Cat."

She didn't hesitate. How could she?

Logan was a man who inspired trust and *she trusted him*. It wasn't like her to invest so much faith in a man she'd just met and the notion scared her spitless. The only way to get through this was to hang on to her heart—and she sensed that wouldn't be as easy as she hoped.

Catherine drew a deep breath and maneuvered herself until she sat in the V of his legs. His warm, solid strength surrounded her, and when his hands wrapped around her waist to better position her, a shot of fire sizzled through her veins.

"Relax. Your headache won't go away if you're still tense."

"Keep your hands there and I can guarantee you relaxing's the last thing I'll do."

He chuckled, his warm breath fanning her neck. "Now hang on." He released his hold on her waist, giving her a chance to breathe easy once more. Then he curled his legs beneath him until he sat cross-legged. "Lie back," he instructed. "Head here." He patted the welcoming space between his knees.

She eyed him warily, but eased her body down until she lay back and propped her head in his lap.

"Okay, now close your eyes."

The last glimpse she got before she shut her eyes was Logan staring down at her with a heart-stopping grin.

"Now breathe deeply and listen to the sound of the fire." As if on cue, the fire began to snap and crackle, sounding louder in the small room. The scent of burning wood filled her nose. And with every breath she took, another muscle in her body seemed to relax and the warmth of the fire seeped inside her. Or maybe it was Logan's warmth and body heat she felt pulsing through her veins. He'd begun to massage her temples with his fingers in soft, gentle motions.

"Now hear the rhythm of the rain." She did. All night the storm outside had matched the one raging inside her.

"Mmm. Don't stop."

"Wouldn't dream of it." He laughed and the sound reached straight down to her toes.

"So tell me how you discovered this...cure," she said, keeping her eyes shut.

"Old childhood lesson." His fingers still worked magic as he spoke. A gentle pressure on her temples, a soft tugging of her scalp. His touch felt wickedly good.

"What do you mean?"

"My sister suffers from migraines. She has since we were kids. She'd get through the weekends fine because my parents were never around, but weekdays were different."

"How so?"

His fingertips moved from the sides to the front of her forehead as he continued to massage. "Weekends they traveled. During the week they were home. Or at least in the state. If they weren't, they'd just come home late and wake us with the arguments they thought no one heard."

And to think, growing up she'd always had the

misconception that money would make things better. She was older and wiser now, but it still hurt to hear that Logan hadn't had an ideal childhood, either.

"That must have been tough to hear."

"Harder for Grace, really. She'd sneak into my room and most times her head was killing her. Stress-induced," he said, the edge in his tone unmistakable.

His obvious love for his sibling was also unmistakable and that was something Catherine could relate to. He claimed to be unaffected by the fighting. She didn't believe him.

"How come they never separated?" she asked.

"Family motto—Montgomerys don't divorce, they endure."

"I thought the wealthy didn't *fight,* they endured," she said lightly, trying to lift the mood that had settled over him thanks to painful memories.

"That motto holds true only in public. For all the money it cost to build the mansion, the walls are incredibly thin."

"So it was you and Grace who did the enduring."

"Yeah. I'd rub her forehead until she fell asleep," he said softly.

His actions toward his sister told Catherine what kind of man Logan Montgomery really was. "I hope she appreciated you," she murmured.

"She did, does."

"I know I do." Another sigh escaped her lips as the gentle pressure of his fingers hit a particularly sensitive spot.

Whatever magic Logan performed for his little sister was brotherly and done out of love. What he did to Catherine was more erotic than fraternal. It was sensual and intimate and she knew seduction was the goal. And she wanted to give in. She had until tomorrow before she had to walk out of this cabin and face the harsh light of day.

Forcing her heavy eyelids open, she glanced up at Logan, wanting to know more about him. "Where is Grace now?"

"Living in a loft in N.Y.C., taking pictures to her heart's content and avoiding commitment for fear of ending up like her parents." He laughed but there was no pleasure in the sound. "She's living off her trust, figuring Mother and the judge owe her for all the misery she lived through."

"Is that how you feel?"

He shook his head. "Actually I live off my salary and not a penny more. If I touch my trust,

I give up control of my life, something I'm not willing to do. And I think Grace would be happier if she did the same." He smiled then, a slow, easy grin that threw Catherine's pulse into high gear and sent out warning signals to every part of her body that wanted to listen.

Judging by her rapid heartbeat, uneven breathing and curling warmth in her belly, no part of her but her brain was paying attention. Even her more rational self wanted to give in to Logan's easy charm and sex appeal, to his understanding nature and giving soul.

"But Grace and her life is another issue for another day. This night belongs to us, Cat. If you want it to." He paused a beat. "The choice is yours."

She sat up too fast and had to wait for the rush of dizziness to subside. When it did, she realized her headache had fled with it. The man definitely had magic hands. The thought caused a delicious curling in the pit of her stomach.

"Feel better?" he asked.

"Much." She sat up on her knees and faced him. "But I suspect that was the point."

"Meaning?"

"You can't seduce a woman if she's going to use a headache as an excuse."

His dark eyes met hers. "I see. And you just admitted yours was gone."

"Completely," she said, the yearning inside her building to unbearable proportions.

The fury of the fire and the driving rain had nothing on the flames burning inside her. But she couldn't help but wonder...

Would one night be enough?

CHAPTER SIX

CATHERINE RAISED HER HEAD and contemplated the importance of the next few moments. He was leaving it up to her to decide whether they would sleep together. Her body said yes, but her mind wasn't sure.

"Whatever you need to know, ask now, Cat."

She grinned. "So you're a mind reader as well as an expert masseur?"

"I already told you I'm a man of many talents. Now quit stalling."

Silence followed. Silence in which no sound but the rain came between them. "There *is* one thing I'd like to get clear first."

"I'm safe," he assured her.

She shook her head. "You're the last thing from safe I can imagine. That storm and those cresting waves are safer than you are. But I understand, and thank you. I am, too, by the way, though that's not what I wanted to know."

"I was afraid of that. What is it?" he asked, twirling a strand of her hair around his finger.

"It's not that I'm asking for promises or anything..."

He stroked a rough hand down her cheek. The caress gave life to a swirling ribbon of need that pulled her in deeper.

"Then what do you want?"

"To know this means more to you than a one-night fling." She met his gaze with a determined one of her own. She wouldn't apologize for her needs.

He treated her to a lazy smile. "Trust me," he said in a husky voice. "It means more. I respect you too much to sleep with you and never call again."

"Now there's a line if I ever heard one." Yet she couldn't help but smile in return. "So what you're saying is, when this is over, you'll call me?" she asked, forcing lightness and humor into her voice.

He nodded. "Soon."

A smile twitched at her lips. "Is that the typical guy version of *soon?*"

His smile vanished, to be replaced by an intense but equally sexy look that set her nerve endings on fire. "It's the Logan Montgomery version of soon."

In the silence that followed, Catherine realized

she couldn't ask for anything more. Either she trusted him or she didn't. And she wouldn't be here if her faith was lacking.

Drawing a deep breath, she met his gaze. "You aren't going to draw this out much longer are you?" she asked at last.

Logan exhaled the breath he hadn't been aware of holding. For a minute there, he'd thought she would bolt. *I'm not asking for promises*. Little did she know he'd have made them willingly. But she had more guts than he'd given her credit for since she hadn't walked out on him just now.

His heart beat rapidly against his chest. Without waiting another second, he swept her into his arms and walked over to the row of windows overlooking the ocean. *His* ocean, *his* beach, the scene that meant so much to him because it represented *his* life. All things he wanted to share with Catherine.

She locked her arms around his neck.

"Take a look," he said.

Turning her head, she glanced out the window. As he inhaled the scent of her hair, his body tightened even more.

"This must be some view on a clear day."

"It's the best."

"It's not so bad now, either." Her eyelids fluttered closed and she tightened her arms around his neck more securely. "You know, all night I've been listening to the sound of the rain."

So had he. The sound of the elements wreaking havoc outside matched the thundering yearning inside his soul. And against his chest, her heartbeat picked up speed, joining his in the same rapid rhythm.

"I live in a one-bedroom apartment. Sometimes, if I'm really lucky, and listen extra hard, I'll catch the sounds of the storm echoing in the night. Otherwise, it gets lost in the blare of car horns and noise."

"I take it you aren't afraid of thunderstorms?" he asked.

She shook her head. "I'm one of the strange people in the world who love the rain."

He closed his eyes and pictured her lying alone in her bed, naked on top of the covers, listening to the pulsing, pounding rain beating against the window.

"Don't you?" she asked.

He forced his heavy eyelids open. "Don't I what?"

"Love the rain? You'd have to to live in a house with all these windows."

"Storms have a beauty all their own." And so did she.

"You have the added bonus of the ocean. The rumble of the ocean mixed with the sound of the waves pounding against the shore. It's electric," she murmured.

"Erotic," he muttered. He lowered her to the floor, slowly, then followed her, feeling her breasts crush against him and the hard peaks of her nipples graze his chest.

He held her gaze fast as their bodies touched and collided, aching and straining with a need that had yet to be met. "God, you feel good." He gripped her waist tighter.

Her assent came out more like a purr of contentment.

"What?" He drove his fingers through her hair. "What do you want?" he asked, resisting the urge to taste her moist lips until he'd heard her say she felt the same things he did.

Her hands gripped his shoulders until her fingernails bit through the T-shirt and into his skin. "I want you to make love to me. I want to feel you inside me, driving me to the edge as hard and as fast as the rain outside. I want…"

Logan didn't wait to hear more. He brought his lips down hard on hers, tasting her, drinking her, needing everything she was willing to give. And her moan of assent told him she'd needed it, too. The music had finished sometime before, and with the storm as their only backdrop, his lips never moved from hers, never letting his body leave her warmth. He hadn't meant for things to get so out of hand, so quickly, but the tempest of desire swirling inside him wouldn't be denied.

Catherine's lower body arched against him, begging, pleading for more. He reached for the bottom of her shirt and sent it flying across the room.

He glanced down and sucked in a deep breath. Rounded mounds of flesh strained upward over delicate peach lace. Her nipples pushed taut and hard against their confinement. The hint of lace he'd seen earlier hadn't done justice to what lay beneath.

He drew in an unsteady breath, then traced the scalloped edging over one breast before lowering his mouth and capturing one of the teasing nipples with his mouth.

Her breath caught, her back arched again and she moaned aloud with pleasure. He couldn't mistake that her body wanted him.

Threading his hand through her feather-soft hair, he brought their faces within inches of each other.

She cupped his face in her hands and covered his lips with hers.

The kiss didn't start out slow. With the desire building all evening, their need was too urgent to contain. Her lips were soft and warm, moist as they opened for his searching tongue, and he swept inside, tasting heaven. And as he'd known all along, one taste wasn't enough.

Gripping her bare waist in his hands, he pulled her closer, wanting to feel her heated skin against his, but his T-shirt prevented him from getting as close as he wanted.

"Here," she whispered. "Let me."

Logan sat back and she pulled his T-shirt out of the waistband of his jeans and eased it over his head. Her soft fingers grazed the skin on his chest. She laughed softly and he knew she'd done it on purpose. "Tease."

She clucked her tongue. "That's not a nice thing to say. I thought you were raised better than that," she said with a grin. "Besides, it's only true if I don't plan to follow through." She ran her hands up his side, letting her thumbs graze his nipples. "And you know I do."

He let out a rush of air. The way she could make his body react with a simple touch defied logic. His erection strained against the rough denim, harder and more insistent with each passing second. He had to regain a semblance of control and to do that, he needed to be *in* control.

"I'm not sure I like that grin on your face," Catherine said warily.

"And I'm just as sure you're going to love it." With steady fingers, considering the circumstances, Logan yanked on the drawstring of her sweats and watched with pleasure as he discarded the loose cotton material. The lacy briefs matched the bra. The tiny scrap of peach material and the hint of what lay beneath made his mouth run dry.

So much for being in control, he thought wryly. But she trusted him, something he didn't take lightly. Logan rose to his feet and before she could question him, he helped Catherine up and swept her into his arms again.

"You really shouldn't make a habit of this. You'll spoil me."

"And that's a bad thing?" he asked.

She laughed. "So what are you doing this time?" she asked, then bit down lightly on his earlobe.

The pull went straight to his already swelled erection and he groaned. "I'm sweeping you off your feet." He tried to ignore the feel of her luscious body molded to his or else he might have come right then, something neither one of them would appreciate. But her soft skin, rounded curves and body heat tested his strength of character.

She rolled her eyes. "I guess I should have told you the first time I don't believe in Prince Charming."

Although her eyes danced with delight, he recognized the sad truth behind her words.

"Then I guess it's up to me to prove you wrong." Before she could respond, he set her down on the couch and knelt down between her legs.

Catherine knew his intent. And suddenly she wasn't so brave anymore. "You know, Logan..." His hands reached for and cupped her thighs. The heated warmth shot straight upward. "Somehow I don't think Prince Charming...had this in mind."

"You know, Cat..." He paused and treated her to a sexy grin. "I'm not sure you'll want to be arguing with me right now." As he spoke, his palms moved forward and his fingers inched higher until they'd reached the edge of her panties.

She let out a whoosh of air. All rational

thought and the desire to speak fled at the touch of his hand. All she could do was feel. The glide of her nearly bare flesh against the leather couch as he pulled her gently downward. The heated, moist sensation of his tongue on her skin. And the white-hot darts of fire and need pricking at her with growing intensity. Everything he did felt right and good.

And when he licked her through the flimsy triangle of fabric, she welcomed the madness that engulfed her. Her remaining inhibitions fled as if they'd never been. She gave herself up to the long, slow strokes of his tongue that alternated with short, teasing flickers and left her wanting and begging for more.

Without her consent, her hips bucked upward from the cushioned couch. He slipped her panties down and she raised her hips to help him, anything to satisfy the aching need. He seemed to understand. After tossing her undergarments onto the floor, he returned to her, and eased his finger inside. She could feel herself moist and wet around him. One finger slipped in and out while his thumb worked at her most sensitive flesh. The tremors began in small waves and continued until they engulfed her in heated convulsions.

And still it wasn't enough. She wanted him with her, inside her and along for the glorious ride. She wanted to see him lose control just as she had. She needed to know she affected him on a level beyond physical need.

With difficulty, Catherine lifted her head off the couch and gazed into his eyes. Desire flared in the brown depths, deeper and darker than anything she'd seen there before.

He rose to his feet. Placing his hands beneath her arms, he helped her rise.

He rubbed his thumb over her still moist lower lip. "I want more, Cat."

"Me, too."

"Still don't believe in Prince Charming?" he asked, turning his attention to the swell of her breast, outlining the scalloped edging of her bra.

"I don't think...what you did qualifies as something Prince Charming would do."

"And why's that?"

"Because as incredible as it was, it's something that's happened during one night of passion. Prince Charming, by definition, is a long-term kinda guy." Now where had *that* come from? The last thing Catherine wanted was for him to run far and fast. She glanced out the window into the stormy night. Especially when he had nowhere to go.

He cupped her cheek in his hand. "We could have more than one night, Cat."

She couldn't believe him any more than she believed in the tooth fairy. Her baby teeth hadn't even gotten her a penny growing up. Neither would useless wishes now. "We're worlds apart," she reminded him.

His arm swept the cottage she'd grown to love in such a short time. "You call this worlds apart?"

Catherine opened her mouth to argue and couldn't. Though the judge's disapproval lingered in the back of her mind, she pushed it aside. Logan was his own man. He couldn't live in this house, work for the public defender, live off his own salary and be anything else.

If he said they had a chance, she believed him. After all, how could she get hurt by class differences when he didn't live them or believe in them?

She wasn't one to give her faith or her heart easily, but Logan made it seem so simple. She reached for him then, gripping his waist in her hands. Hot muscle pulsed beneath her fingertips causing an answering tug deep inside her, in areas he'd already loved thoroughly.

Trouble didn't begin to describe what she'd

gotten herself into. She glanced into Logan's warm eyes. She couldn't give him anything less than the truth. "I call this making my dreams come true."

With a harsh groan, he swept her off her feet again, only this time she didn't argue and she found herself lying on the rug in front of the fireplace. He removed his jeans. He wore standard white briefs, but nothing could look ordinary on a man with his physique. Broad shoulders, flat stomach and bronzed skin, he was a perfect male specimen down to the bulge she couldn't possibly ignore, even if she wanted to.

He placed his hands on the waistband of his briefs, and never taking his gaze from hers, he drew them down until he was naked, then he stretched out beside her. The swell of his erection pressed against her thigh and the warmth of shared body heat was sweeter and hotter than the blazing fire he'd created.

If this was what it felt like to *believe there existed a chance for them,* Catherine was suddenly glad she'd opened her mind to the possibility.

"I've only just begun," Logan said. He lay beside Catherine, flesh to flesh and discovered her skin was softer, her body warmer than he'd imagined.

"To what?" she asked.

"To make those dreams of yours come true."

"You make me think anything's possible," she murmured.

He switched positions, easing himself over her until he lay on top. His arms prevented his weight from crushing her, but their lower bodies fit perfectly. His erection, hot and heavy, settled between the V of her legs.

"That's because it is," he told her.

Her eyelids fluttered shut and a soft moan escaped her lips. Logan nearly came right then, but somehow he didn't think that's what she had in mind. Besides, he'd promised to make *her* dreams come true. His be damned.

With one hand, he cupped her breast. She fit perfectly in his hand. Her skin was supple, in direct contrast to the rigid nipple pressing into his palm. Logan kneaded her waiting flesh, savoring the fullness nestled in his hand. With his thumb and forefinger, he teased her taut nipple, plucking, rolling and flicking the erect nub until she writhed beneath him.

He stared at her face. Green eyes stared back at him. He placed a kiss on her upturned nose and then did the same to the tip of her breast.

"Who's the tease now?" she asked in a husky voice.

He answered by running his tongue in a circle around the white skin on her breast, coming to a halt only after flicking the tight nipple with his tongue. He raised his head and grinned. "Complaining?" he asked.

"Only that you're not inside me already."

"That's not a complaint, it's a request."

A soft smile played on her lips. "Take it any way you want," she said on a soft sigh. Her hips jerked upward, whether on purpose or an involuntary response to pure desire, Logan didn't know. Nor did he care.

He just knew the time was right. He transferred his attention from her breasts to the warm, moist place between her legs. He wasn't surprised to find her wet with desire, hot with the same aching need that burned inside of him. It was the same desire that had flared into an inferno within him the second he'd laid eyes on the beautiful bartender. Logan's gut told him it wouldn't be satisfied with just one night of abandon. Even if his body were to be sated for the moment, he *knew* he would crave more of her.

He separated them long enough to reach for his jeans, and the condom he'd shoved into the pocket earlier, just in case. In case he were lucky enough to have one time with this one woman.

Unable to wait another second, he glided into her slick heat with a hard and demanding thrust meant to let her know exactly what she did to him.

Filled and fulfilled. Catherine wondered if she'd ever understood the distinction before. Logan grasped her hands and intertwined their fingers together above her head. The uniting motion ground their bodies together until they weren't just joined, they were one. Thoughts like that could only lead to pain and disaster, yet with Logan staring into her eyes, she couldn't think negative thoughts.

She couldn't think at all. His lips covered hers in a kiss as hot and promising as the heat between their bodies. Between them, they began a grinding, rocking motion that was sweeter than it was fast, more reverent than it was frenzied. If Catherine had made love before, she couldn't recall. Because anything less than this was sex and this was so much more.

He released her hands and braced his on either side of her shoulders. "Look at me."

She did, and saw a raw need so deep, so exposed, she was swept away by it. Words failed her but emotion didn't. He'd drawn her in, deep and fast.

With every gliding motion, he came fuller and

deeper inside her. The tip of him was smooth, but with every thrust she felt the rougher ridges of his erection and the friction was almost unbearable.

Her eyelids fluttered shut. He kissed each until they opened again and then he began a rhythm unlike anything she'd experienced before. Sleek and measured one minute, he created an agony so prolonged and exquisite she wanted to cry out for harder, faster, pounding thrusts. But when he answered her silent plea, her body built toward completion too fast and she missed the drawn-out intimacy they'd just shared.

Just when she was about to topple over the precipice, he slowed the pace once more until her body begged for completion. But Logan was in control and he wasn't giving in. Wasn't letting it happen fast and easy. Wasn't letting this be an experience she'd put behind her anytime soon.

The fast and furious pace slowed. "Open your eyes."

She hadn't realized she'd closed them. "What do you want from me?" she asked him.

"Everything." And then he thrust so deep she was sure they'd been joined for eternity. He moved inside her and she raised her hips, allowing him even fuller and deeper access, heightening her pleasure.

Catherine couldn't look away from his deep, compelling gaze. No doubt that was his intent and the crescendo came without warning, a tidal wave beyond her control.

THE AFTERSHOCKS STILL rippled through his system. He doubted he'd ever breathe normally again. Logan rolled to his side and glanced at Cat who looked as sated as he was. Her cheeks were flushed pink, her green eyes were still heavy-lidded and her breathing still sounded rapid and shallow.

He stretched his arms overhead. Huge strategic mistake, he discovered immediately. Catherine rolled onto her back, away from physical contact. That cleared his mind at once.

If she needed distance, he respected that. But not until she understood a few things. He'd never lost himself with someone before and he'd have bet she felt the same. He closed the gap between them and wrapped his arm back around her.

She didn't pull away but instead surprised him by curling into him. "That was incredible," he whispered in her ear.

"Mind-blowing," she agreed.

He hoped she was referring to the emotion involved as much as the act itself. He waited a beat but she didn't speak. Apparently she needed space. Her next words confirmed it.

"It's getting cold in here, don't you think?"

"I'm pretty warm myself." He nuzzled the side of her neck.

Her laugh sounded more relaxed. "You know what I mean."

He did. Once she drew his attention to it, the crackle of the fireplace called to him. "Tell you what. Let me put out the fire and we can move to the bedroom."

He held his breath. After the intimacy they shared, now wasn't the time for her to be claiming the couch for the night.

She nodded. "Sounds good."

Giving her some distance and privacy, Logan rose first and grabbed for his jeans before kneeling by the fire. It wasn't easy, knowing she was undressed behind him, but somehow he managed.

He wasn't great at reading signals women sent out, but he sensed she needed a combination of space and reassurance. Just one of the many things he liked about Catherine was her honest responses.

Logan feared, given the chance, she'd run from what they shared instead of facing it. He'd finally found the one woman who liked everything in his life that was real and nothing that was related to the Montgomery wealth or status.

If he had his say, she wasn't going anywhere anytime soon.

CHAPTER SEVEN

CATHERINE WOKE TO THE SUN streaming in through the window. Logan's window, Logan's room. She glanced over, but his side of the bed was empty. The shower sounded in the background. She lay back into the pillows. Every pull of her muscles reminded her of last night. And, Catherine admitted to herself, she felt good.

At first, she'd been afraid of the aftermath, afraid he'd find himself with a woman he'd had enough of. But when she'd rolled away, giving him the option of space, he'd rejected it. Everything before and since had been like a dream.

She'd been so depleted she barely remembered making her way from the den to the bedroom, and after he'd returned from putting out the fire, she'd curled into his warmth and fallen fast asleep.

There hadn't been time nor energy for second thoughts then, but she had plenty of opportunity now. Yet the one thing she couldn't do was regret her night with Logan. He'd been a generous and giving lover, attuned to her wants, her needs and her feelings. But it did figure.

The only one-night stand in her life and she had to pick the wrong man. Oh, he was the right man in every way—just not for her. She was petrified their worlds would collide and destroy what they had shared.

The jarring ring of the telephone shattered her thoughts. Good thing, since she didn't like the direction they were taking. She let it ring, until the answering machine on the bedstand clicked on and she heard Emma's voice say, "Logan? Cat? Come on, pick up. I know you're there."

Groaning, she reached for the phone. "Hello?"

"Too tired for an amusing greeting. That must be a good sign."

"Emma." Catherine laid her head against the pillow. It was no wonder Logan had nearly given up trying to keep up with the older woman. She probably had more stamina and antics up her sleeve than the two of them put together.

"So glad you recognized my voice, dear. Long nights can sometimes cloud the brain. How are you feeling this morning?"

She refused to succumb to the bait. "Just fine, Emma. And you?"

"Just fine means my grandson's technique needs work."

Catherine felt a heated flush rise up her naked body. Logan's technique had been beyond amazing, not that it was any of Emma's business.

Catherine wondered how long it had been since anyone had given Emma a run for her money. She adored the older woman, but a lesson was in order.

"You know, you're right," Catherine said. "Maybe it was the long drive or the run through the rain, but he just wasn't up to what I'm sure is his normal…potency."

Emma coughed. And Catherine realized the bathroom door had already opened, in time for Logan to have caught the end of the conversation. He stood by the bed, his jeans riding low on his narrow waist, a towel hanging over his shoulders, and an eyebrow raised in blatant disbelief.

"Emma," Catherine mouthed, pointing to the receiver.

Logan placed a finger over his lips, and motioned for Catherine to hand him the phone. She nodded and did as he asked. He held the receiver in one hand and hit the speaker button with the other.

"You do realize sometimes men aren't up to snuff their first time with a woman, but I'm sure it'll get better, dear."

Catherine couldn't help it. She burst out laughing.

Emma sniffed. "I know you're there, Logan, and speakerphones are so rude. Have I taught you nothing about class and refinement?"

It was Logan's turn to laugh. "Everything I learned, I learned from you. Didn't anyone ever tell you it's rude to pry?"

"I was just having a nice conversation with Catherine, wasn't I, dear?"

Catherine bit down on her lower lip. "Yes, ma'am. But you should know I stayed because of the storm. Nothing happened last night." She crossed her fingers behind her back as she spoke.

But at the mention of last night, Logan's steamy gaze met hers. "Liar," he mouthed as he lowered himself beside her on the bed.

The distinct masculine scent of spicy soap and aftershave aroused her in an instant. She pulled the sheet up around her, but the effort was too little too late. He'd already seen it all, and more.

"Well, of course, nothing happened. I raised my grandson to be a gentleman. And you're every inch the perfect lady. For *him*," Emma added.

"Now I've got to run. I'm hanging up now, bye." A click was followed by a long dial tone.

Logan snapped off the speakerphone and they both laughed aloud.

"I wonder if she learned her lesson," Catherine asked.

"Doubtful. You wouldn't believe the last plan she had in mind for us."

"Us?"

He nodded. "Emma had a plan before there even was an *us*. She was born to scheme."

Catherine grinned. "Apparently so. But she also had a strong influence on your life and your character."

"Tell me how you figured that out," he said wryly.

"Well, aside from the obvious, I'm observant." She glanced around her again, at the room in which the Logan Montgomery, bachelor, lived.

"Almost everything here is your distinctive personality. The wood furniture is old but masculine, like the brown and tan color scheme. The wood's not polished, it's worn and comfortable. But there are touches in here that you'd never have chosen on your own. Touches I'd bet Emma supplied."

He grinned, obviously amused. "Such as?"

"Well, a man doesn't go for the little things. That throw rug by the bed? It adds warmth to the room. The tray with your keys on the nightstand? I bet you'd just toss your keys on the dresser. You'd never think of buying a pewter tray. And those antique books and the shiny marble bookends? A gift," Catherine said, fairly certain she was correct.

At least, she hoped she was. She preferred to believe his grandmother had supplied the decorative touches than to think he made a habit of bringing women to his cottage on the water.

"You're partially right. Emma bought the rug and the antique books."

"And the rest?" she asked, holding her breath.

"A beautiful woman with too much money to spend supplied the bookends and the pewter tray."

A twisting jealousy churned Catherine's stomach and she didn't like the feeling. "Well, she's got good taste," she admitted grudgingly.

"She should. Her feisty grandmother taught her everything about having a decorative eye. Grace was a fast learner," he said, laughing.

"You're a rat."

He eased himself beside her. The mattress dipped beneath his weight. Before she could think, he leaned forward and brushed a warm kiss over her lips. "But I'm a lovable one."

He was right. "You're an arrogant rat," she said, refusing to let his ego swell.

"So Grace says."

"How often do you see her?" Catherine asked.

"Not enough. But we check in once a week, usually Sunday nights. I like to make sure she's not getting into trouble, and she likes to keep up on life in Hampshire. Even if she won't admit it out loud, she misses her friends here. She even misses certain members of the family."

"You and Emma." It wasn't a difficult guess for Catherine.

"And Mother. Believe it or not, she and Grace have this bond. It's Dad she can't stand to be around."

"Maybe she'll come home one day."

He shrugged. "A lot of things would have to change." His gaze met hers, zeroing in and not letting go. "But you never know. Miracles do happen."

A tingling sensation took hold, and Catherine breathed deeply. His potent scent made her stomach curl in response. "What time is it?" she asked.

"Ten."

"Wow!"

"I take it you're not used to sleeping in?"

"What can I say? You wore me out."

He grinned. "I'll take that as a compliment."

Reaching behind her, she grabbed for her pillow and playfully hit him on the shoulder. "You would."

"I also kept my first promise."

She raised an eyebrow. "And what would that be?"

"Since it's morning, we've had more than one night." His boyish grin disarmed her defenses.

For a woman who didn't believe in much, he was awfully close to making her believe in the promises he made. *We could have more than one night, Cat.* The man believed in miracles. How could she discount his promises?

But her mother had believed her father's promise that he'd stick around—and he had—long enough to make two children as soon as biologically possible before disappearing for good. Logan wasn't a man like her father. Thanks to his grandmother, he was grounded in reality. Any man willing to take on the commitment of a mortgage and a run-down house knew how to settle down and grow roots.

Not that she was foolish enough to expect anything long-term from Logan Montgomery. Or so she told herself. But Catherine feared if she spent much more time with him, she'd begin wanting just that.

"The sun's out," she said inanely. "I really do need to get to my sister's." Out of here. Back to reality. Where her practical sister and her know-it-all cop husband could give her a good mental shake and remind her why she *could not* believe in the fantasy she had begun to weave.

"I was thinking we'd go out for breakfast and I could drop you off after."

Catherine bit down on her lower lip. She'd regret this later, but he deserved something kind from her. "Tell you what. Give me a few minutes to shower and I'll fix you something here. Then you can take me to Kayla's."

"That sounds good." He leaned closer. His lips were in kissing distance again and she waited. "But the cupboards are bare," he said softly.

"I wish we were." She bit her tongue the minute the words escaped her lips. "I mean, that's too bad."

He grinned. "Not really. This way I get a rain check."

Catherine opened her mouth to argue and this time he sealed his mouth over hers, cutting her off.

At least for now.

AFTER FOLLOWING CATHERINE'S directions, Logan pulled up in front of a quaint house painted in a light shade of gray. The sun bathed the house in light, now that the rain and clouds of the day had dissipated. The half hour drive had passed quickly. Cat had chattered during the entire trip and Logan now knew all about her sister, Kayla, her husband and their soon-to-be expanded family.

Catherine obviously loved her sister and, despite her complaining, he sensed she liked her sister's husband. He also believed Catherine rambled out of nervousness, because she didn't want to discuss the possibility of seeing each other again.

She didn't believe they had any sort of future and Logan intended to prove her wrong.

In Catherine, he detected a deep sense of longing for the hearth-and-home type of life her sister now had, even if she'd never admit it aloud. He recognized Catherine's yearnings because they echoed his own need for desires he never realized he'd had. Until Catherine.

"Well, we're here."

Resting his arm over the steering wheel, he turned to look at her. "Yes, we are." He noticed her hand on the door handle and grinned.

"Going somewhere, Cat?"

Her blush would have charmed him, if she hadn't already had him well in her grip. "Home?" she said.

"Without a word?" Teasing her came naturally, if only because she took it so well.

She opened her mouth, then closed it again.

"Say so long," he instructed her.

She shook her head. "I have no idea why I let you fluster me," she muttered. "No one flusters me. Not even Nick."

"Who's Nick?" he asked, hating the sound of another man's name on her lips.

"My chef. And close friend. We went to culinary school together. He's been teasing me since he was shorter than me and after I kicked him in the shins the first time…"

"He never tried it again?"

Catherine laughed. "Of course, he did."

"And this Nick. He's a…"

"Friend," she said softly. Seriously, as if reading the tone in his voice. "An engaged friend. He hasn't made a move since we were kids."

He met her steady gaze and knew he'd been right. She'd understood and sought to reassure. He appreciated her for that. He'd never succumbed to jealousy before but wasn't surprised his first time involved Catherine Luck, because no woman had ever affected him the way she had.

She uncrossed her legs. "Goodbye, Logan." She looked away, and before he realized her intent, had pulled on the door handle.

"Cat, wait."

She released it and turned. Her green eyes were suspiciously damp. "What?"

"Goodbye's too final." Myriad words were on the tip of his tongue, but goodbye wasn't one of them. She'd be seeing him again, whether she believed it or not.

She drew a deep breath. "It was fun, but…"

"It was more than that."

She shook her head. "It can't be."

"Why? Because my name's Montgomery?"

"That's one reason." Catherine didn't dare name any more. Otherwise she'd risk admitting her real feelings and the fact that she was dangerously close to falling in love with a man she'd just met.

Love at first sight didn't exist. Once she got out of this car, she'd remember that.

"This is the modern world, Cat. Class differences don't exist."

Tell it to the judge, she thought, but refused to utter the words aloud. Logan had gone so far out of his way to distance himself from his family and their way of life, that Catherine knew he believed what he said. He just didn't realize what would happen when two worlds like theirs collided.

Besides, she had no doubt that once he got back home, all she'd be to him was a distant memory. "Can't we just say it's been fun…"

"And I'll see you around?" he jumped in, finishing for her.

"Something like that."

He grinned and she knew she'd dug herself in deep. "Sounds good to me. I'll pick you up Friday. We'll have dinner in Boston before driving back to the beach. Maybe this time the weather will be nice and I'll get to show you some of the more special spots hidden away from prying eyes."

He'd gotten the best of her and he knew it. "You're too literal," she told him.

"I'm honest," he shot back. "And you led me to believe you valued that quality."

"I do," she whispered.

Nothing like her own words to sway a wary heart, Catherine thought. Unsure of what else to say, she gripped the door handle tighter.

"Then believe me when I say I want to see you

again. There's something too strong between us to just let it go."

Her heart began a rapid, pounding beat inside her chest. He was good with words—hers, his, it didn't matter—because he was even better at getting past her defenses and making her believe in the impossible.

She glanced outside and saw her sister's husband, Kane, walk out the front door. Probably making a routine check on a suspicious car in front of his house, Catherine thought wryly.

She had no desire to introduce these two men and endure Kane the detective's probing questions later. "I have to go."

"Friday?" he asked. "You owe me breakfast," he said when she remained silent.

She gazed into his eyes. His honest eyes. She'd made love to him, opened up to him and she trusted him. The only person she was fighting here was herself.

A smile tugged at her lips.

"You're wearing my favorite sweats and I'd like to collect them in person." He was persistent, she'd give him that. He had no way of knowing she'd already made up her mind.

"Call me," she said and before he could

respond, she opened the door and slipped out of the car, slamming it behind her.

"Ball's in your court," she murmured aloud.

He didn't know where she lived, nor did he have her number. Of course, thanks to Pot Luck and Emma, she was easy to find. But if he was truly interested, he'd have to make the effort. She wasn't coy nor was she playing hard to get. She just wanted to know he was serious before she allowed herself to get in any deeper.

Problem was, Catherine was in way over her head already.

"*THE* LOGAN MONTGOMERY? You slept with *the* Logan Montgomery?" Kayla's voice seemed unnaturally loud in the small bedroom.

Catherine cringed. "Would you stop saying it like that? And what do you mean *the* Logan Montgomery?"

Her sister reached for the stack of newspapers lying on a table beside the bed. "It's in here somewhere. In today's 'Living Large' column…"

"Hold on." Her sister was beyond intelligent. She read fiction, literature and medical journals, but… "You're reading gossip columns? Stop the world, I want to get off."

A red blush stained Kayla's fair skin. "Ever

since the doctor said bed rest, I feel trapped. I go through books like they were water. Even Kane and his library trips after work can't keep up with me. I'll read anything, including trash," she admitted.

Catherine sat on the edge of the bed and patted her sister's hand. "What's it like to live in the common world?" she teased. Kayla was smarter than any person had a right to be and she had an incredible memory. She could spend hours in a library, reading material of interest to no one else in the world.

"Very funny." Kayla thumbed through the newspaper. "Aha. Here it is. Take a look."

Knowing she wouldn't like what she saw, Catherine accepted the paper anyway, and found herself face-to-face with a close-up shot of Logan, taken at yesterday's Garden Gala. Even at a distance, his good looks were enough to take her breath away. But the memories of their intimate moments, the sound of his deep voice, his warm hands on her body, *him* inside her...was enough to melt her heart.

"Read the article," Kayla said.

Catherine shifted her attention back to the paper. "Favorite Hampshire man, Logan Montgomery, son of Judge Edgar Montgomery and his wife, Annette, is rumored to be ready to announce his candidacy for mayor of Hampshire. Although the delectable bachelor firmly denied the story, Judge Montgomery told this reporter to stay tuned—as if any of us need an additional reason to keep an eye on this perfect specimen. Too bad for us single working girls, he's destined to be snapped up by..."

Catherine crumpled the paper and tossed it on the bed. "I can't read any more of this trash."

"Oh my God, you've fallen in love with him." Kayla eyed her through narrowed eyes.

Catherine shook her head. No way she'd admit those feelings, not even to herself. She couldn't leave herself that exposed, open, raw... "What am I going to do?" she wailed and tossed herself across the foot of Kayla's bed.

"You could start by cleaning yourself up."

Catherine rolled over and glared at her brother-in-law who stood in the doorway.

"Go away," the sisters said at the same time.

"You know you only say that when she's around," he said to his wife.

Catherine grinned. "At least I make you suffer, too, McDermott."

"Before you two get started, can I get a word in edgewise?" Kayla asked.

Catherine sighed. She'd met Kane right after he'd slept with and used her sister. At least that's what Catherine had believed, and though Kane had proven himself since, the sparring and bickering from the early days remained a part of their relationship. Catherine held a grudging respect for the detective, stemming from his devotion to her sister, though she'd never admit it aloud.

"Go ahead," Catherine said to her sister.

Kayla turned to her husband. "Cat needs a place to think…"

"I do?"

"And she's going to be staying here until she settles some things."

"She is?" Kane asked. From the narrowing of his eyes, the thought didn't please him.

Catherine grinned. "I am," she said and folded her arms across her chest. Until Kayla said the words, Catherine hadn't realized how badly she needed her sister's advice or how much she didn't want to be alone with her thoughts.

She glanced at Kayla, tucked safely under the covers, her large stomach protruding through the sheet. She was due in a matter of weeks and there was no place else Catherine wanted to be when the baby came.

Kane walked over to his wife's side. "Don't you have work at home?" he asked Catherine.

"I can drive home, get the books and play catch up from here. No parties until next weekend. Our new manager is handling Saturday's affair. I've got Sunday. So it looks like I'm here to stay."

"Swell," he muttered only to be greeted by Kayla's elbow in his side. "I mean, make yourself at home. But no redecorating while you're here."

"A man who doesn't like animal prints has a fundamental problem relating to life," Catherine told him. "They add warmth..."

"That's what live pets are for," Kane muttered.

"All my accessories are fake. I'm a strong believer in animal rights. But if it's a pet you want, I can stop by the pound..."

"I'm leaving," he said to both sisters.

Catherine grinned. "That was the plan. But seriously, Kane, thanks for the place to stay."

"You're welcome." He graced Catherine with a genuine smile.

"I appreciate it. I could really use the company."

"Stay as long as you want. Just keep out of my way."

"He doesn't mean that," Kayla assured her.

"Sure I do, sweetheart…when I'm alone with you," he said in a deeper tone, one a husband reserved for his wife.

To Catherine's surprise, a pang of envy darted through her heart. She'd spent a lot of time with Kayla and Kane, happily married couple. Through Thanksgiving, Christmas and other assorted holidays, Catherine had felt joy her sister had found love, and acceptance despite Kane's outwardly surly attitude. But she'd never envied what Kayla and Kane shared. Never thought she wanted it for herself.

Until now.

Until Logan.

Hampshire's favorite man.

The delectable bachelor destined to marry wealthy and within his class, she thought, recalling the final words of the article. The words she couldn't bear to read aloud.

CHAPTER EIGHT

LUNCHTIME ON MONDAY, Logan stood at a pay phone in the courthouse. From the minute he'd gotten into the office this morning, his boss had had him at his beck and call, covering an important case for a hospitalized co-worker, when the judge refused to grant a postponement.

He dropped in money, dialed Catherine's phone number in the city and listened to the incessant ringing before the answering machine picked up. He muttered a curse. His only break for the day that would give him free time away from the client, and Catherine wasn't there.

"Montgomery, Judge wants you in his chambers. Seems your client's causing trouble again," the bailiff called from across the hall.

Logan groaned, slammed the receiver down and with a regretful glance at the phone, he ran down the hall.

Sometimes priorities sucked, he thought.

HIDING OUT WASN'T SMART. It didn't say much for her ability to cope. But then, Catherine didn't want to cope. She wanted to forget. That she'd slept with Logan. And that he hadn't called.

She'd arrived at Kayla's on Sunday and today was Tuesday. So what if she hadn't told him where to reach her? He was a lawyer. A smart guy. If he'd wanted to find her, he could. Easily.

As much as she'd told herself not to expect anything, that she didn't want anything, his silence hurt anyway. Because despite all the truths Catherine knew in her mind, her heart wanted to believe she was different, special. Not just a cheap and easy fling.

She wanted to forget, and catering to her pregnant sister would help her do just that. Plus, it would allow Kane to leave the house without worrying that he'd left Kayla alone. It was the least she could do in exchange for invading his space and their privacy. She carried a tray of food upstairs and knocked on the bedroom door.

"If it's more muffins, I'm stuffed."

"Cinnamon French toast," she called back and kicked open the door with the toe of her foot.

Kayla propped herself up in bed.

"I made it just the way you like. A few raisins, a touch of low calorie syrup..."

"Cat, sit down."

After placing the tray on the dresser, she joined her sister. "I'm sitting. What's wrong? Is it the baby?" She glanced at Kayla's stomach and was rewarded by a jolt of movement under the sheet. "Active little guy."

"Or girl. Listen to me. About all this...food."

"I've been cleaning the kitchen, I swear. And I'm freezing the casseroles. You and Kane will have enough food to get you through the..."

"The first decade of this child's life. Catherine, slow it down. I know you better than anyone. You only cook like a demon when you're upset. It's been two days and you haven't mentioned him but you've barely left the kitchen."

"Him who?" she asked, avoiding her sister's gaze.

Kayla rolled her eyes. "You know stress isn't good for the baby." She patted her stomach. "And worrying about you is stressful. Now stop playing dumb and tell me what gives."

Trust Kayla to hit her in the heart. Catherine eased herself down on the bed. "Remember when we were kids? And Christmas came? All the kids on the block got tons of gifts. Even if it was a used bike or a hand-me-down doll, they got wrapped gifts under the tree and Santa came."

"But not for us," Kayla said softly.

"Right. How many birthday wishes and Christmas lists did I waste asking for my daddy to come home?"

"I'm not sure. You never said it out loud. You swore it never bothered you the way it bothered me. And I should have sensed that it did."

Catherine shook her head. "There you go again, taking responsibility for things you can't control. If I didn't admit it, I didn't *want* you to know."

As she met her sister's gaze, Kayla motioned for her to continue.

Catherine bit her lip. "It took me a while, but after the first couple of years, I caught on. He wasn't coming back...and I stopped believing."

"In more than just Santa Claus," Kayla said.

Catherine nodded. "And then I met Logan. I knew we were from different worlds. I knew I was just an interesting diversion. And yet..." To her horror, tears filled her eyes and she brushed them away with the back of her hand.

"You believed in him."

She nodded.

"Then don't you think you should have given him your home address? Your phone number?"

"I know this sounds awful but I think...I thought if he had to work at it, I'd know he was sincere. It wasn't difficult. His grandmother knows exactly how to reach me."

"Have you called your machine?"

Every hour on the hour. "Yes. And nothing. Besides, he dropped me off here. At the very least he knows how to find you." She shook her head and dismissed the subject with a wave of her hand. "Forget about it."

"He could just be busy with work."

On call three nights a week and one weekend a month... "It doesn't take long to make a phone call." To find out *where* to pick her up on Friday. For the date that wasn't going to happen.

The ring of the doorbell cut off her train of thought. "Expecting company?" she asked her sister.

"Could be Kane's boss's wife. I mean, old boss. He retired last year. She stops by every week with...more food," Kayla said with a groan.

"I'll get it. Just remember, no one cooks like me." Catherine forced humor and lightness into her voice as she walked out of the bedroom and headed for the door.

If Catherine was going to stay, she needed to give her sister support and not stress. Neither one of the sisters knew how to turn off their motherly instincts toward the other. They were too deeply ingrained for too many years.

On the other side of the door was a delivery man and not the captain's wife as Kayla had predicted.

"Delivery for Catherine Luck."

She narrowed her eyes. "That's strange."

He shrugged. "Are you her? I need a signature."

Catherine scrawled her name and accepted the small box covered in plain brown paper wrap. Turning the square box over, she found the return address, written in an unfamiliar scrawl.

She'd never seen his handwriting, she realized. How many other things didn't she know about Logan Montgomery? Too many. And yet the small box that fit into her hand filled those gaps until they didn't seem to matter.

As she tore into the paper, Catherine hoped with everything in her that it wasn't an illusion.

LOGAN TOSSED HIS KEYS onto the metal desk, kicked aside the garbage can and unloaded armfuls of folders onto the floor. His desk was piled high with files and paperwork that ought to keep him busy straight through next year. He muttered a curse. Add to that Tuesday night calendar where he represented whatever case came onto the docket, and the result had been no time to himself.

Zero time to sleep...or to get in touch with Cat, though he'd continued to try. Having gotten her number from Emma, he'd called her during court breaks, but he'd gotten her machine each time. After the closeness they'd shared, what he had to say couldn't be summed up in sixty seconds, and that was all the time he'd had, considering he'd been handed this case cold on Monday morning.

The burning desire to see her again was all-encompassing. Everything about her appealed to him. Her allure...her uncertainty.

He'd promised to call her "soon." That was Saturday. He'd dropped her off on Sunday. And here it was Tuesday night. He rubbed a hand over his burning eyes and picked up the phone. He dialed, it rang and the machine picked up yet again.

He hung up the receiver. "Son of a..."

And got hit in the head. "Didn't I bring you up better than to curse like that?" his grandmother asked.

He stared at the open door she'd barged through without warning. "And didn't Emily Post teach you to knock?"

"Why should I? Door's open."

He hung up the phone, rose and walked around his desk. "Good to see you, Gran. You're always welcome. You know that." He kissed her weathered cheek, wondering why she would show up at his office at this hour of the night.

"Of course I do. But it wouldn't matter if I wasn't. We need to talk." The gleam in her eyes intrigued him as much as it disturbed. She was up to something again.

"How'd you get here?" he asked.

She let out a long-suffering sigh. "I let Ralph drive me. Though I still say that DMV person was wrong and I am not a hazard on the road." She sniffed.

He'd never let her know that after she'd backed over her prized roses in the driveway, *he'd* pulled strings to make sure she had an eye exam and didn't get her license renewed. He wanted her to live as long as possible. "Well, I'm glad you were prudent anyway," he said, knowing she still snuck a drive or two when she could get away with it.

"Like I had a choice. Your father would call the cops on me. His own mother. Imagine that."

"Imagine." He grinned. "I have to call Cat first and then we can talk."

CARLY PHILLIPS   165

She glanced warily at the phone. "Talk first. Call later," she said, sounding panicked. "I haven't eaten. Let's go to that fancy place downstairs."

"That fancy place is a bar."

"Sounds good. Let's go." She yanked his arm. For a frail-looking woman, she had almost super-human strength. Although he could argue with her, he had no desire to make his first call to Catherine with an audience present and he knew damn well he'd never get Emma to wait outside. Better to feed her and send her on her way. *Then* he'd call Catherine and leave a message if he had to.

He managed to grab his folders and stuff them into his briefcase before she herded him out the door. Five minutes later, he and his grandmother were seated in a sports bar in the same building as his office.

"Want to see a menu?" he asked her, calling the waitress over at the same time.

She shook her head. Not a strand of white hair fell from her perfect bun. She hadn't changed since he was a kid. And he loved her for it, even if there were times—like now—when she confounded him.

"Whatever you're having is fine with me."

He rolled his eyes. "Beer, and I thought you hadn't eaten."

She fidgeted in her seat. "I lost my appetite."

"Two beers," he said to the waitress.

"Be right back."

Logan leaned back in his seat and glanced around the crowded bar. "Okay, you've got me in a public place where I can't make a scene. What's going on?"

"You are good."

The waitress returned and placed two bottles and their glasses down onto the table.

"I'll take mine straight up," Emma said.

He swallowed a laugh.

"You might want to do the same."

His urge to laugh ceased as he digested her warning. He handed her one bottle, grabbed the other for himself and took a large gulp, refusing to comment when she did the same. The sight was absurd but no doubt that was her intention. Get him in a public place, keep him off guard and drop her bomb, whatever it was.

The cold, wet brew didn't ease the dryness in his mouth. "Now tell me what's going on."

"What? I can't stop by to visit my favorite grandson?"

"I'm your only grandson. Now talk."

She sighed. "You're working hard?" she asked.

"It's been a hectic week."

"And it's barely begun. No time for play?" she asked.

"You keeping tabs on me, Gran?"

"I have to hunt you down at your office at ten o'clock…it speaks for itself." She tilted her head to the side. "The women in your life can't be too understanding if you're so out of touch."

There are no women in my life, he almost said. It was his standard response to Emma's not-so-subtle prying. But he caught himself because they both knew, this time, it would be a lie.

As much as he valued his privacy, he wouldn't mind unloading on Emma. She understood him better than anyone else and already knew he was interested in Cat. More importantly, she liked Cat, too.

He leaned forward. "I'm not sure how she feels about me right now. I haven't been able to reach her."

"Haven't had time, you mean." Emma made a chiding, clucking sound with her tongue. "You know what they say about all work and no play. You ought to go find Catherine and have a good time with her. Relieve some of that tension you're carrying around with you."

He had no patience for her prying, or the way

she spoke of Cat as if she meant nothing more to him than a good time in bed. He shook his head. "You cut that out now," he warned his grandmother.

She clapped her weathered hands together. "Thank goodness."

"Thank goodness what? Someone other than the judge is finally censoring your language?"

"Logan, I raised you, I love you, but you can be thick as a milkshake sometimes. Thank goodness you're looking out for Catherine. If you don't let me talk like that about her, I picked right and *it's* finally happened."

"Your train of thought boggles the mind," he muttered. "But I'll bite. What's finally happened?"

"You've fallen hard. I knew you would. Now here's the plan." She talked fast, probably before he could interrupt. "When I realized you were tied up for two days, I took a few liberties."

He shook his head. She was a whirlwind and, right now, his life was caught dead smack in the middle. "Which reminds me. We still haven't talked about the closet incident."

"Oh, I thought you and Catherine already taught me a lesson," she muttered.

"So you didn't like being on the receiving end, did you? Now listen and understand. Much as I appreciate your intentions, your…meddling can't go on. I'm thirty-one years old, Gran. Would you take it personally if I said butt out?"

"Of course not. But it's too late for that. You need the scoop and I'm here to give it to you."

"And I'm here listening."

"You said at the party you wanted to make Catherine's dreams come true. And before you ask how I know, I accidentally left the intercom on by the pool house where the bar was located," she said, unable to meet his gaze.

He blinked hard. "You're telling me you sat in the house and listened?" he asked, buying himself time to swallow his anger.

"Yes," she admitted with embarrassment and shame in her tone.

Emma wasn't malicious nor did she ever mean any harm. But the knowledge didn't help right now. He closed his eyes and counted to ten, attempting to control his frustration. The penalty for murder in this state wasn't pretty and even though this could be considered justifiable homicide, the jury might take exception to the fact that he'd strangled his eighty-year-old grandmother.

"I only needed to know if I chose right," she said, by way of explanation. "If you two hit it off. Heaven knows you'd never tell me the truth."

"Only because you react...like this." He balled his hands into tight fists. The thought of her invading his and Catherine's privacy had him seeing red. "You might mean well, but you passed the bounds of common decency this time."

"Actually, I know that and I'm sorry." She bowed her head. "But that heart attack scared me to death. Well, not literally, thank goodness, but it meant I had to see you settled down and happy before I passed on. Went to the great beyond. Well, you know what I mean."

He did. And he understood. Her heart attack had taken years off his life as well. And the reason he let her get away with so much interfering was because he loved her and was grateful she was still around to meddle in his life.

But she couldn't go to these extremes, not when Catherine was involved. "I already told you I won't use Cat in any scheme to stop the judge. You should be ashamed of yourself. You claim to like this woman and you set her up, plan to use her..."

Emma rose to her feet, indignation in her posture and the determined look on her face. "I did no such thing."

"Sit down, Gran."

She lowered herself back into the booth.

"Well, I set her up with you, if that's what you mean. But you should be grateful. As for using her, can I help it if her background will infuriate your father and thwart his mayoral plans? But that has nothing to do with why I brought you to the party. I wanted you to meet her. Period."

"And if we didn't hit it off?"

"I'd have backed off," she said, with the utmost sincerity.

Logan ran a hand through his hair. If the past two days of work hadn't been enough, he now had this to contend with. "Then do it. Now." He imposed as much authority into his tone as possible without being disrespectful to the woman he loved.

She patted his hand, much as she'd done when he was a child. Through the years, the gesture had been oddly comforting. But now it made him wary and her next words proved his instincts were on target.

"There's just one more tiny little thing."

"IT'S ROMANTIC, CAT." Kayla beamed and it wasn't just the glow of pregnancy lighting her features.

Catherine knew her sister was thrilled by Logan's daily gifts. No more than she was herself.

She stared down at the three gifts laid out on the bed, finding herself at an uncustomary loss for words. Logan did that to her, she thought, warmth spreading through her.

She shook her head. "I don't know what to say."

"You wanted sincerity. Looks like he's given it to you."

Catherine nodded. A different box had arrived every day. A box of fairy dust on Tuesday. The card read; To Make Your Dreams Come True.

On Wednesday a snow globe. To an outside observer, the gift held little meaning. But the scene inside depicted canoeing on the Charles River— and a gentle shake showered the boats in falling snow. Snow in the summer time. And she remembered the words on the card: Miracles Do Happen.

He was her miracle and she was enveloped by the aching desire to feel his arms around her. Oh, he was good. The right gifts, the right words. A subtle, mental seduction, she thought. Did a man go to those lengths for one more night of sex?

Making love, her heart said. And that's where they were headed if she went with him tonight. The third gift that arrived this morning was proof of that. A CD. The jazz music from the night they spent in each other's arms and another note: Until We Can Be Together Again.

She fingered the smooth plastic disc holder and a different desire kicked in this time. The need to have this music, their music, filling her ears at the same time he filled her body. A shot of desire rocked her hard, and she wrapped her arms around her stomach to stop the trembling.

"Cat? Cat? Are you okay?"

"What?" Her sister came into focus. "Oh, yeah. I'm fine."

"Where did you disappear to?"

"I'm sorry. I just don't know what to think. These gifts are…"

"Sweet? Thoughtful? Stop trying to put a word on it and go with what you feel."

Catherine laughed. "I remember telling you to do just that before your first date with Kane."

Kayla grinned. "And look where it got me." She spread her hands across her large stomach.

"If you're trying to scare me, you're doing a good job." But she couldn't deny the thought of being Logan's wife, having his babies, held a strange appeal considering the short time in which they'd known each other.

She shouldn't rush things. He wanted

another night. Never had the long-term future been mentioned.

"Oh, come on," her sister said. "Tell me you don't want this." She spread her arms out in a broad sweep. "The husband, the love, the security...the house, the kids..."

"The dog and the white picket fence? Get real, Kayla. This is me we're talking about, not you. I don't inspire a man to thoughts of permanence." Of course, she'd never considered a future with any of the men she'd met, either, until now.

"Oh, and you think I did? Before Kane, what did I ever get out of a guy except it's been fun, see you around sometime? Why don't you believe that one person exists who was meant for you? That you deserve it all?" Kayla asked, pure frustration in her voice.

"Because I'm not an incurable romantic like you. And even if I was, we're talking about Logan *Montgomery* here. You didn't see that house. I'm sorry, that mansion. The coat closet was bigger than our room growing up."

"So? You said his house was your dream cottage. And before you start in, I have an answer for every argument you can throw out."

"Except this one. Can you see me as the

CARLY PHILLIPS   175

mayor's wife?" Catherine stood and gestured to
her outfit, the clothes she'd picked up from her
apartment the other day. With a black T-shirt,
white jeans and leopard-print sandals on her feet,
she wasn't exactly the demure type.

"I can see you as the mayor's unique wife, yes.
I can also see you adapting. But as I recall, Logan
denied the rumors. Cat, he's pursuing you. He's
obviously not concerned about these things. Why
are you? The past is behind us. You're more than
worthy of him...unless you're looking for an
excuse to steer clear," Kayla guessed with dead-
on accuracy.

"Would you please have this baby already so
you'll have something else to worry about besides
me?" Catherine muttered.

"I could have ten kids and I'd still worry
about you."

"I know." Tears filled her eyes. Without Kayla
she'd have no one.

She told herself she wasn't foolish enough to
believe Logan was in it for the long haul. She
glanced at his thoughtful, sentimental gifts. No
matter how much her heart disagreed.

CHAPTER NINE

CATHERINE DIDN'T HAVE to wonder what she wanted from Logan. He'd made certain of that.

She wanted *him*.

Every gift, with every note, had led her to that conclusion. When all her thoughts were consumed with him, what else could she possibly desire? She shook the globe and watched the snow shimmer and fall on the summertime scene.

And after listening to the low strains of the jazz CD all afternoon, her heart throbbed in time to its beat, and her body yearned for his touch. She was beginning to believe he was right and that they had a chance.

He hadn't called. No doubt that, too, was calculated to heighten her sense of anticipation. It worked. By the time the doorbell rang, Catherine didn't care about backgrounds, class, money...or anything except being with him again. Because not only had he seduced her, but he'd also chipped away at the wall she'd erected to keep him at arm's length. He'd reached her heart—from a distance, at that. Heaven help her, now that he was here.

Kane beat her to the door. Greetings bought her time to calm her raging nerves. By the time she made her way downstairs, the two men were deep in conversation. They'd probably discovered they had the law in common, even if Logan did work to spring the men Kane put behind bars. Good thing they worked in separate jurisdictions, Catherine thought wryly.

She caught sight of him the second her feet hit the floor of the small entryway. She took in his tight jeans, navy-and-white striped shirt pulled taut over his broad shoulders, day-old razor stubble and nearly lost it right then. His penetrating gaze met hers, deep and knowing. He looked at her as if he could read minds, as if he knew her most secret desire.

He held her gaze and winked. Catherine drew a deep, shuddering breath. Because she saw it in his eyes. His feelings mirrored her own.

Although he continued to talk to Kane, Logan held one hand out toward her. No sooner had she come within touching distance, than he snagged her hand and linked their arms together, drawing her close. His skin was warm, his touch possessive and welcoming. She thought she'd calmed the flutters in her stomach but they returned full force.

She'd never had a father to greet her dates and she felt twice as ridiculous now, at the thought of making small talk with Logan and Kane. She cleared her throat. "So. I see you two have met."

Kane nodded. Logan opened his mouth to speak.

"But we haven't." Kayla's voice sounded from the top of the stairs and cut him off.

"You're supposed to be in bed," Kane growled, but Catherine heard the affection laced with concern in his tone.

"And I suppose one of you was going to bring Mr. Montgomery up to meet me?" Kayla asked, knowing neither she nor Kane would have done any such thing.

"It's Logan. And it's nice to meet you, Kayla." Logan grinned. He couldn't mistake the resemblance between the sisters despite Kayla's obviously fuller and very pregnant form.

"And now you can get back in bed," Kane ordered. He turned to Logan. "Doctor's orders," he explained.

"No, your orders. You know darn well he said

it's safe for the baby to come any day and I can move to restricted activity."

Kane held out his hand and Logan shook it. "Nice to meet you, Montgomery. I'm going to carry my wife back to bed."

"I'd like to see you try," Kayla called back.

Catherine's laughter sounded in Logan's ear, as sexy and arousing as he'd remembered. Obviously she was used to this byplay. Logan wasn't. Not once had he seen his parents so obviously happy together.

But he had that chance. Thanks to Catherine, they had that chance—to see where this thing between them led.

Before Kane hit the top step, he called out, "Montgomery."

Logan glanced up.

"Hurt my sister-in-law and you answer to me." Seconds later, Kane had swept his very pregnant wife off her feet and into his arms. As they disappeared down the hall, a door slammed shut behind them.

Logan understood Kane's warning. He accepted it without malice. But he doubted Catherine would appreciate her brother-in-law's interference. Yet when he met her gaze, instead of anger, he saw wonder and disbelief.

"I thought he put up with me for Kayla's sake," she murmured in answer to his unspoken question.

Her reaction hit him in the gut. Had she always felt so alone? He knew the answer because he often felt the same. One more thing they had in common. One more thing he wanted to change in her life.

Without thinking, he pulled her into his arms. "There you go again, selling yourself short. I won't have it, Cat."

"What will you have, Logan?" Her eyes glittered with pleasure.

Pleasure he wanted to increase. "You." His hands moved and cupped her waist. Because her ruffled shirt ended at the waistband of her fitted black pants, his hands gripped bare skin. Logan let out a slow groan.

She sucked in an answering breath before meeting his gaze. "Say that again."

He glanced into her green eyes and recognized her need to be reassured. Their week apart had worried him and he saw now he'd been right to be concerned. He curled a strand of her hair around his finger and tugged lightly. "I want you, Cat. All of you."

She sighed softly. The sound went straight to

his groin, stopping first to wrap itself around his heart. She surprised him by moving closer. Their lower bodies collided and a shaft of white heat shot through him, hard and fast. No way could she mistake his body's reaction.

He glanced at her, expecting to see remnants of self-doubt in her gaze. He saw only clear certainty. Unabashed desire.

For him.

He'd never been more relieved. When Emma had informed him she'd sent Catherine a gift...fairy dust, of all things, he'd nearly had a coronary. Of all the corny, harebrained schemes, with this one, Emma had outdone herself. But as she'd informed him, he could spend his time yelling or pick up the ball she'd dropped and run with it.

He still wasn't taking his grandmother's calls and was barely speaking to her, but he'd chosen to run with it. Once his eighty-year-old spitfire interfered, what else could he do?

Catherine wasn't one for expensive gifts or flowers. She wasn't impressed with money or material things. Honesty had reached her once before, during the closet episode. He hadn't forgotten that.

When he'd left her at her sister's she'd been wary and skittish. If he wanted to reach her again, he had to sway her mind first. Her body he had no trouble with, he thought wryly. So, taking quick breaks from work, he'd come up with the other two gifts, choosing to let his words speak for him.

Apparently he'd been on target, he thought as her hands pulled his shirt out of his jeans and her palms splayed against his back.

"I think we ought to move this someplace else," he said and she nodded.

Heartened, he asked, "Are you ready to let yourself believe in possibilities?" Because he didn't want just another night with regrets in the morning.

The week without her had been hell. And if this thing between them had happened fast, he was willing to let it take the lead. He'd had too many other weak imitations of what he and Catherine shared not to recognize its potential.

But she had to be open to the future, too. He couldn't pursue this alone. He held her and waited.

"I believe in you," she admitted, her heart in her eyes.

He'd be a fool not to know what the admission cost her. And it deserved one from him in return. "I was thinking we could go home."

She tilted her head back to meet his gaze. He kissed each eyelid and then her upturned nose. "My home," he added. "And there's something I want you to know. You're the only woman I've ever brought there, Cat."

Before she could answer, he brushed a kiss over her soft lips. He meant to reassure, but the fire flared fast and without warning. Breaking contact wasn't easy but he managed.

She let out a shaky laugh. "You do have a way with words, Mr. Montgomery."

"I do, don't I?" he said with grin. "Now let's go home."

THE COTTAGE LOOMED in the distance, as warm and welcoming as she'd remembered it. Logan pulled in front of the small house and cut the engine. With the sun setting behind them, Catherine followed him inside. Desire throbbed inside her as fast as her rapidly beating heart. But the one thing she was aware of was a sense of belonging.

Deprived and lost were the only words Catherine could think of to describe how she'd felt the week without Logan. She'd known him one day. It felt like a lifetime, maybe because he'd used that week wisely, to build faith. Trust. Longing.

The minute the door to the cottage slammed closed behind him, all those feelings came rushing to the surface. She wasn't sure who turned first, who reached for whom first. It didn't matter because his arms were around her and his mouth came down hard on hers. She welcomed the firmness of his lips and the sweeping thrusts of his tongue because she'd been deprived for too long.

She ran her fingers through his hair, holding his head, silently pleading with him not to stop. Not to leave her. He groaned and pulled her closer, aligning their bodies so she could feel him, hard and full, throbbing against her. Liquid heat pooled inside her and trickled between her legs.

She whimpered and he moved his hand and cupped her intimately, knowing and anticipating her need. "Logan." Somehow, she found the strength to separate their lips.

With an agonized groan, he met her gaze. But he didn't move his hand and his thumb rubbed in lazy circles over the soft denim covering her, until her breath came in shallow gasps and the dampness increased.

"What is it, Cat? Tell me what you want."

She wanted the ache to ease. The throbbing to stop. And she never wanted it to end.

She wanted him.

She tipped her head back and realized she was braced against the wall, her legs bracketed between his strong thighs. He stared back at her with a heavy-lidded gaze. "Talk to me," he murmured.

But one of his fingers was tracing her moist lips and the sensation was both sensual and hypnotic. Clearing her mind wasn't easy. She wasn't even sure why she needed to, but it had to do with explanations and what he thought of her. "I don't...I mean I'm not usually so..." Her voice trailed off as his wet finger moved from her lips to her jaw, to her collarbone, settling finally in the soft V of her top, enfolded in layers of ruffles.

His gaze never left hers and that same finger pushed down on the elastic, exposing her breast to his heated gaze. Her stomach muscles contracted with need and her nipples tightened at the first rush of cool air.

He sucked in a ragged breath that matched one of her own. "It's never been like this for me, either," he muttered.

Was that what she'd been about to say? She wasn't sure and it didn't matter. Not when he was right. When everything was so right.

And that was the problem. Nothing had ever felt so good, so perfect...so meant to be. How was that possible? Life didn't work that way. It didn't give something so wonderful, not without taking away in return.

"Don't think, Cat. Not now." He cupped her chin in his hand and tilted her head for a gentle kiss. A hard demanding one would have been more welcome. She could have handled want. Sweetness and understanding might be her undoing.

After her lifelong protests, and years of disbelief, she felt herself being swept away, succumbing to the fantasy. The one she'd buried and the one he wove. The happily ever after one. She shivered in outright fear.

He grabbed her shoulders for support. "We'll talk all you want. Later."

After he'd bonded them together again, Logan thought. After he'd reminded her of how good they could be—if only she'd let herself believe.

Her sigh was one of acceptance. He knew because she leaned toward him, not away. Because her hips bucked against his painful erection. And because she leaned forward and whispered, "Yes," in his ear.

Only then did he let himself look down at her full breast filling his hand. "You're not wearing a bra," he muttered. Her breast, heavy and hot filled his palm.

A warm flush rose to her cheeks. "It's not like you can see anything through the ruffles."

He grinned. "But I've gotten way past the ruffles." He brushed his thumb over one tight peak and felt the pull straight down to his own groin. He dipped his head for a taste.

Her unique scent filled him as he pulled the tight bud into his mouth. He flicked and teased with his tongue, then his teeth, until her hips rocked so insistently against him, *he* was in danger of losing control. Beyond thought or reason, he reached for her snap and somehow he remembered to grab for protection. Then between the two of them, her pants hit the floor, then his, and their underwear followed.

He turned and grabbed for her once more. He lifted her. "Wrap your legs around me, sweet-heart." She did and as he lowered her onto his waiting erection, her body took him deep inside.

He'd known she was wet and hot, but the glide into her slick heat was as easy as it was sweet. A muffled sound broke through his ecstasy. He opened his eyes in time to catch a lone tear drip down her cheek. He recoiled immediately and tried to back off. "I'm hurting you."

She shook her head. "Not the way you mean," she whispered. "It's a good hurt."

The constricting in his chest eased. Her legs grasped him tighter and her wet muscles contracted around him. He let out a groan. "Baby, I know what you mean."

He met her gaze, grateful to see her smiling this time. Leaning forward, he licked the salty tear off her cheek. The motion had the effect of grinding their lower bodies together. The wave crested and eased. Her soft sigh told him she'd felt it, too.

"Logan?"

"Hmm?" he asked through clenched teeth.

"Any slower and I might have to strangle you."

"You have to admit, it's a helluva way to go."

She yanked back on his hair and he grinned.

"Easy, babe." But despite his soothing words, his body was hammering for release. And she'd just given him the okay.

What came next defied anything in his experience. He'd meant to move but she beat him to it, and what he'd expected to be an in and out satisfying of their bodies, turned into a rocking, twisting motion that had the effect of drawing him into her, body, heart and soul. The tempo increased and she bucked and undulated against him, and he against her until the swaying and twisting had his body reaching...cresting... peak-ing on a wave of something so strong, so deep, everything inside him was swept away.

WHEN HAD SHE FALLEN ASLEEP? Catherine blinked into the sunshine streaming through the open blinds. She stretched and felt the protest in muscles she'd overused last night. It felt decadent to wake up in Logan's bed after the endless hours they'd passed here. It felt even better to be entangled in his arms. He'd tossed one leg over hers, as if to lock her in place. She laughed. It wasn't as if she was going anywhere, she thought. Not until noon when she had to head home and get ready for the party Pot Luck was supplying the decorations for tomorrow. As parties went, this one was simple because it just required setup.

"Something funny?" Logan asked.

"You're up."

He grasped her hand and edged it downward. "In more ways than one."

His deep voice wrapped around her. "You're bad," she murmured.

"And you love it." In one smooth motion, he rolled over her, bracing his weight on both hands.

She loved... Oh, no. No way. Not so soon. Not now. Not this man. She scrambled to get away, but his lower body held her fast. And the

more she squirmed the more their bodies con-
nected. The more his solid erection pressed tight
against her. Hot, pulsing, liquid heat spread
through her.

"Stop squirming, Cat." His voice was deadly
serious. "Now before something happens you
obviously don't want, why don't you tell me
what has you spooked?"

She stopped, then shook her head. She may
have bared her body to this man but no way
would she bare her soul. She couldn't give him
that kind of power over her.

"Okay, how about I tell you what has me
spooked. You can go next."

"Sounds fair." And it would give her time to
regain her equilibrium and come up with something else to tell him. Anything was better than the
truth.

What a joke. Catherine Luck, daughter of a
supermarket clerk and a man she didn't even
remember, in love with Logan Montgomery, son
of the most powerful judge and family in the
state. If she wasn't careful, the hysterical laughter
she felt bubbling to the surface would turn into
buckets of tears. And Catherine never cried. Not
since the Christmas she'd realized Santa was a
fraud and her father was never coming back.

"Look at me."

She forced herself to gaze into his handsome face. The only way to conquer her fears was to overcome them. She'd done it before, she could do it now. The smile she faked was more difficult. "Okay, you go first."

"You're running from me. No matter how deep I dig, no matter how honest I am, or how much of me I reveal, you run the other way."

She couldn't deny it. Not only did he open up verbally, but he didn't hold back when they made love, either. Catherine had limited experience. But even if her sexual past was uneventful, she was smart enough not to think that an earth-shattering experience between the sheets had any meaning outside the bedroom. Her mother had done that. Head over heels in love with a man who wanted her in bed and no place else.

She shook her head. That wouldn't be her fate.

"I'm not running from you, Logan. I'm..." She thought of everything she could say and opted for the truth. "I'm running from the result."

He rolled to his side. "Back to that again, are we? The differences? The idea that we won't last?"

She couldn't deny that, either. "Yes."

"Okay, we'll play it your way. One day at a

time. It works, it works. It doesn't, it doesn't. That make you feel any better?"

His compelling eyes stared into hers.

"No," she admitted.

"Good." He treated her to a heart-stopping grin. "That tells me you care."

"I do," she said softly.

His gaze softened. "There's something to be said for that honesty of yours."

"And any man who can send the gifts you did deserves at least that in return. You care about my dreams, Logan." And it may not last forever, but it certainly touched her heart, Catherine thought.

His gaze darted away from hers. She couldn't read his expression but he was uncomfortable and that wasn't like him. "What is it?"

"I do care about your dreams. Don't ever think I don't. But…"

"But?"

He ran a hand through his already disheveled hair. "Hell, do you think a guy would send you fairy dust?" he muttered.

"You didn't?"

He shook his head and she felt her heart squeeze tighter. "The globe—the snow in the summer?" she asked.

"That was me. So was the music. And the notes that came with both."

The constricting pain in her chest loosened. "But the fairy dust?"

He rolled his eyes, then covered them with one arm. "Emma," he muttered. "And if you have any sympathy for me, you won't ask how she knew us so well."

Catherine nodded. She wasn't sure she wanted to know that herself. "So she wants us together?" she asked.

"It would seem so."

That was a piece of this puzzle that hadn't made sense to her from the beginning. Why would Emma Montgomery, no matter how eccentric or outlandish, seek out a woman like Catherine for her beloved grandson?

Catherine had done well for herself. She didn't deny that; in fact, she was proud of all she'd accomplished. But she knew good and well where she came from. And she certainly knew her family wasn't the type to gain points with the illustrious Montgomerys. Forgetting that she came from the wrong side of the tracks, she knew only too well that the recent past hadn't been kind to the Luck family, either.

Not only had her aunt married a man with

mob ties, but he'd dabbled in prostitution. To make matters worse, they'd been killed and left their charm school—a front for her uncle's prostitution ring—to Kayla and Catherine. And the entire sordid story had played out on the front page of the papers. There was no way anyone who lived in the state of Massachusetts and was breathing at the time would have missed the juicy tidbits in the news.

Logan hadn't mentioned it, but maybe he was just being the gentleman he'd been raised to be. And as long as he didn't see fit to mention it, she didn't plan on discussing that bit of family humiliation, either.

"I don't get it," she said aloud.

He ran his hands through her hair. As always, the light tug on her scalp sent her senses soaring.

"Don't get why she'd like you?" he asked.

She didn't want to have this conversation. "I'm a likable person," she said lightly. "I can just think of more suitable women she should be throwing you together with. I couldn't name any of them, of course—I don't run in those circles. But it doesn't make sense that she'd go to all that effort to matchmake between us."

"It makes perfect sense to me." His warm breath tickled her cheek. "We make perfect sense to me."

Since she'd seen so much of Emma in Logan—his charm, his personality, his determination to do his own thing—Catherine could almost believe Emma, too, found them a perfect match.

His cheek rested against hers. A silly little thing, but just feeling him that close caused an answering need to soar through her. And when he spoke about them as if there were no barriers, no constraints...she wanted so badly to give in to his seductive words and unspoken promises. Without realizing it, she rolled closer, until their bodies aligned once more.

"Your turn, Cat." His voice was a hoarse command. And she felt him hard against her.

He wanted her. She wanted him. What was stopping them?

"Your turn," he said again. "Tell me what's bothering you."

Catherine smiled. It wasn't difficult considering Logan was gazing into her eyes with genuine concern. How could she not have fallen hard?

But she knew what was stopping them and it was plain old common sense. Hers. Just because she'd fallen didn't mean she had to let him know it. "Nothing's bothering me except that I'm starving."

"I don't believe you," he whispered in her ear. "But I'm hungry, too."

"Good. Then lie back and relax, and let me do all the work. I promised, remember?"

"Only if you promise to take a walk with me afterward. I want to walk on the beach with you. And I want you to talk to me."

"You drive a hard bargain, Mr. Montgomery."

He grinned. "It's part of my charm."

He was charming, all right. But during the time she'd known him she'd learned a little bit about semantics and wordplay. He said he wanted her to talk to him. She'd agreed.

But it didn't mean she had to tell him what was in her heart.

CHAPTER TEN

LOGAN LOCKED THEIR HANDS together and led her onto the beach. The sand was still damp from the early morning and felt cold and wet beneath his feet—unlike his body which was hot and bothered. She'd satisfied his hunger for food, but not for her.

Catherine had whipped up a meal unlike any he'd ever had. He was impressed not only with her talent and ability to make a feast out of the meager offerings in his kitchen, but with the pure enjoyment the task gave her. This wasn't a woman who demanded to be waited on or who expected maid service just because his last name was Montgomery.

"So tell me about your plans to run for mayor," Catherine said.

"What makes you think I'd run?"

"I heard you mention something about it when your father picked up the phone last week, and I read it in the paper," she admitted.

He stopped walking. Catherine kept on going until his resolve and his firm pull on her hand stopped her. She turned back to face him.

"How do you feel about that?" He didn't mean to hedge, but he needed to know what she was thinking. He studied her, but had a difficult time reading her neutral expression. He let the silent moment go on.

The roar of the waves crashed in the background. The light breeze blew her hair around her face and carried with it the scent of saltwater from the ocean. He inhaled deeply. In this spot, he'd found the sense of peace that had eluded him all his life, so buying the house had been the logical thing to do.

When Catherine's wide green eyes met his gaze, the same feeling enveloped him and he knew. In this woman, he'd found that same elusive contentment. She, too, brought him peace.

She shrugged. "What you do—whether you run for mayor or not—is none of my business." But the intense look in her eyes was at odds with her words.

"Let's get something straight. From this moment on, if it involves me, it involves you. That's what *us* means." He tugged on her hand and drew her against him.

Her full breasts pressed against his bare chest and he let out a groan. Thanks to the ample privacy the beach house afforded, neither one of them was fully dressed. His cutoff shorts were his only concession to clothing, while she wore one of his oxford shirts and the skimpy underwear he'd peeled off her the night before. Taking advantage, he slipped his hands beneath the shirt and laid his palms on the soft skin of her back.

"Us," she murmured. "I do like the sound of that. You make life sound so simple."

"That's because it is. But for the record, I'm not running for office. It isn't me."

She smiled. "I happen to think you'd do a great job, but I agree." Her hand reached up, and she brushed his hair off his forehead.

The simple gesture, sweet in its simplicity, was oddly sensual, too. His body, already on edge, stirred to life.

"The stuffy public image of a politician isn't you."

"I'm glad you know me so well. If only my father did, too, we wouldn't even be having this conversation," he muttered. But Judge Montgomery had never known his only son, except as an extension of himself. He'd never even bothered to try.

And it hurt. The same part of Logan that rebelled against the family dictates also longed for a normal father-son relationship. One he'd never have.

"I take it you've told him?" Catherine asked.

"Over and over. He won't accept it, which means he continues with his own agenda. At least until I come up with a way to stop him."

"You want him to accept more than your decision not to run for mayor, don't you?" she asked. The light breeze blew her hair into her face and she held it back with one hand.

"You know that I do. I suppose it's human to want parental approval."

"It's not just that. You've accomplished so much with your life that you've earned that approval. Unfortunately he's withholding it because your needs don't meet his needs. It's sad, really. And you're both missing out."

"You're perceptive. Anyone ever tell you that before?"

She shrugged. "Not really. I think it's just because I've come to know you so well, that I can read your feelings."

He grinned. "So I've accomplished a lot in a short time."

She rolled her eyes. "Leave it to you to make this about us. Now what about your mother?"

Catherine asked. "Can she be counted on to bridge this gap? Did you ever take your case to her?"

He shook his head, amazed he'd never thought of it before. "For so long I've seen her as an extension of the judge, the one who carries out his wishes in public. But really I don't know much about them or their marriage in the past few years." And though he rarely allowed himself to dwell on his lack of family life, he did miss things about his mother.

She lifted her shoulders. "Maybe it's time you learned."

"You're a wise woman, Catherine Luck."

"An even wiser woman once told me that women are smarter than men and I shouldn't ever forget it. Perhaps I've just proven her right," she said with a grin.

"If it's Emma you're talking about, please don't ever give her the satisfaction of letting her know she's right about anything. She'll be impossible to handle."

Catherine laughed. "She already is. And maybe if you get things resolved through your mother, you can get Grace to come home." She touched his cheek. "Because I know you'd like that, wouldn't you?"

He grasped her wrist and looked down at her solemn face. She cared about him and his family. And he cared about her.

"Yes. And I'd like to know what's going on in that head of yours even more."

She wrapped her free hand around his waist. "Nothing worth discussing, I swear."

"Trust me, sweetheart."

"This has nothing to do with trust. And just so you know, it's not that I don't trust you."

"I know. You don't trust life not to throw you a curve."

A grin tugged at her lips, making him want to lay claim to that luscious mouth. "You're beginning to know me very well, too," she said.

"I'm glad." They'd gotten far enough for now. He glanced out over the ocean. Deep blue for as far as the eye could see until in the distance the horizon appeared, a sky of light blue and cotton puffs of clouds. "Have you ever seen a place that offered pure peace?" he asked, hoping she'd see his haven as he did.

She tipped her head to get a better view. "It's beautiful here. Not just the water, but the cottage, and the silence. It's bliss," she murmured.

He nuzzled the soft skin of her neck. "So are you." And he wanted as much time with her as he could get before her work intruded. He glanced at his watch. "It's nearly ten. We have an hour before I have to drive you back."

He slid his hands from her back and cupped her unrestrained breasts in his hands. Their fullness and weight pressed against his palms.

She swallowed a moan. "An hour. That's a long time."

He dipped his head and caught her mouth with his for a long, mind-drugging kiss. As his tongue swept inside, his hands caressed her breasts and rubbed circles around her taut nipples. Without warning, her hips bucked against his, teasing his straining erection and testing his tenuous restraint.

Coming up for air wasn't easy, but he managed. He had to if he wanted to get her back to the house. "I'm not sure an hour's going to cut it. Not with what I have in mind."

Her already flushed face deepened a shade and her eyes glazed over with desire. She looked like a woman who'd been kissed hard and loved well. Meanwhile he felt like a man on the edge, who hadn't had nearly enough.

"What did you have in mind?" she asked.

He grabbed for her hand. "Race me back to the house and you'll find out."

SHE MUST BE OUT OF HER mind. This man who held her hand so tightly, who cherished her with his gaze, his touch, his words... She trusted him. And if her mother had believed in her father... well, Thomas Luck wasn't anything like Logan Montgomery. Her father wasn't a hardworking, loyal, upstanding kind of guy. No one was more distrustful than the Luck sisters, but even Kayla had ultimately believed in a man. In love. In the future.

Maybe it was time Catherine did the same.

She ran with Logan down the long stretch of beach. The wind whipped through her hair and she inhaled the tang of saltwater with every breath. Now that she'd opened both her heart and her mind to the possibilities, everything before her looked fresh and new.

By the time they reached the house, Catherine was out of breath and laughing hard. Her laughter died quickly when she caught sight of the fire still burning in Logan's gaze. The intensity was catching and a blaze erupted deep inside her. Her heart began a steady pounding, one that echoed in her ears.

"Cat." His voice was a deep, husky rumble.

He grabbed her around her waist, hiking the oxford shirt up around her thighs. Laughing, she reached for him with one hand—and then a flash went off in front of her eyes. They weren't alone.

"What the hell?" Logan reacted first and shoved her behind him, blocking her from view. Considering her state of undress, she appreciated his chivalry but the picture had been taken and his gesture came too late.

"Mr. Montgomery, I'm here to meet you and your supporters as you announce your candidacy for mayor of Hampshire." The female reporter glanced at her watch. "I thought the press conference was set for ten but…"

"Press conference?" Catherine asked, stepping out from behind the shield of Logan's body.

"Yes. Judge Montgomery said it was at ten, though I may be mistaken."

"Would it matter?" Logan muttered. "You just got your scoop."

Catherine yanked down on the hem of Logan's shirt. It barely covered her thighs and she'd never felt so vulnerable and exposed.

"You said this press conference was planned?" Even as she asked the question, her heart turned ice cold.

"For the past week. And you are…?"

"Find out on your own," Logan said, then

turned to Catherine. "Let's go inside. We need to talk."

She would have swallowed but her mouth was dry. "I'm not sure there's anything to say," she told him.

"Can we discuss this in private?" He gestured toward the eager reporter and her camera-toting sidekick.

Without glancing in their direction, she walked ahead of him and headed for the safety of the house. No sooner had he closed the door behind them than he grabbed for her hand. "Cat..."

"I'd rather you didn't."

"Touch you or explain?"

She turned to face him.

Perhaps he read her emotions on her face, because he'd schooled his own expression into an unreadable mask. "I take it the answer is both." Pain and betrayal flashed in his eyes, because she wouldn't give him the opportunity to set things right.

"I'm not sure an explanation would make any difference," she said. He'd never know the answer hurt her as much as it obviously hurt him. And her heart, which had been as warm as the sunshine, was now frozen solid.

This type of life wasn't something she understood, nor did she think she could get used to being in the public eye. Hounded by the press. Caught in varying states of undress and embarrassment.

"Well, tough, because you're going to listen. After all that's passed between us you owe me that."

She nodded. "I'm listening."

"The way I see things, the judge orchestrated a meeting here because he knew I wouldn't show up at *his* designated spot. Since he knows nothing about you—us—I don't see this as anything more than a very bad coincidence."

Logan's worst nightmare, actually, but Catherine didn't seem as if she'd be receptive to his feelings at the moment. Not when her own were so obviously hurt and raw. He felt for her, but he also had a heart and, by ignoring his attempt to explain, she was trampling on it.

She sighed and tugged on the bottom of her shirt. He couldn't begin to imagine her humiliation. Because of him. Hell, he'd dig into his trust fund if money would prevent that picture from being published. But it wouldn't. Good press was worth more to the vultures out there than cold, hard cash.

"I can see your father's manipulation in all this and I'm sorry he's still trying to control you."

Pain still danced in her eyes, along with what looked like resignation. "But I'm not sure I can stick around and be fodder for the press." She glanced down at her bare legs, and he remembered her shirt hiked over her panties at the time the photo was taken. He shuddered at her humiliation.

"Cat…"

"I also think I see your grandmother's hand. She locked us in a closet and she sent me things calculated to make me fall in l…to make me fall for you."

He raised an eyebrow at her near slip. Now *that* was something he wanted to pursue further. So was his grandmother's possible role. The fact that Emma had suggested this very scenario wasn't lost on Logan.

But he wasn't willing to give up on Emma yet. "I admit she had her own agenda. I even mentioned it to you the other day. But setting you up was never part of her plan."

For all her faults, the older woman had a huge heart and she obviously cared for Catherine. Logan had no choice but to take a leap of faith and believe in Emma's integrity. Otherwise every good thing about his childhood and his life had been based on yet another illusion.

Catherine wrapped her arms around her waist. "Whether it's Emma or your father who called out the press, it doesn't matter. I just want out of here before this becomes a media circus."

He muttered a curse, unsure what her feelings were behind the wall she'd erected. He didn't have time to find out because she was right. He had to get her out of here and fast.

A glance out the window revealed a black sedan pulling into the graveled, unpaved space in front of his house. As usual, the older man's appearance was timely as well as unwelcome. Logan rubbed his hand over his eyes and groaned.

He hoped this glance at his reality gave the judge a much needed eye-opener. He'd certainly gotten one. For all his talk of being his own man, he was still having his strings pulled like a damned marionette.

But it would stop. Today.

Anger and frustration pulsed through him, as strong as the desire he'd been feeling minutes earlier. The last thing he wanted to do was give Catherine a way out of his life. But he owed it to her. If he wanted any shot of winning back the heart he'd worked so hard to reach, he had to let her go now.

He grabbed the keys to his truck he'd left hanging on a hook in the front hall. "I'm parked just outside the door. Walk out and don't talk to anyone. Don't answer any questions. Just jump into the car, circle around whoever else has arrived and keep driving."

Her sad eyes met his. "Thank you."

Why did those two little words sound so much like goodbye? He glanced at her parted lips and the need for one last taste zipped through him.

He reached for her, grabbed her forearms and pulled her close. She didn't draw back, but the playfulness was gone. So was the unguarded look. Instead of her heart in her eyes, she now had it firmly under lock and key.

A loud pounding sounded on the door. Logan lowered his head and brushed his mouth over her lips. She tasted sweet and a renewed desire to reclaim his life—and her—surged through him. She sighed and he deepened the kiss, sweeping his tongue inside. The knock came again, louder this time.

She jumped backward. He didn't blame her but still held her tight. "I open the door, you slip by him and keep going. Got it?"

She nodded.

"This isn't over, Cat. *We* aren't over."

"You're too much of an idealist," she murmured, touching his cheek.

He shook his head, reaching for the door at the same time. "I'm a realist, and when this is over, you'll be part of my reality." He turned the knob. "Now go."

He opened the door, expecting her to duck past the judge without a word. Instead she paused in front of him.

"Hello, Judge Montgomery."

His father looked flustered for a moment, as his gaze darted from Catherine to the waiting reporters. "Miss…"

"Luck. Catherine Luck."

Logan wasn't concerned that she'd given the judge her name. The papers would print it anyway. But he grimaced in disgust at his father's snobbery. She'd catered a party in his house and the judge, master of working a room, couldn't be bothered to remember her name. But now he would. Logan had a hunch after today, Catherine Luck was a name Judge Edgar Montgomery would never forget.

She held out her hand and, after a brief hesitation, the judge accepted her greeting. "Do I know you?"

"I catered your party last week," she reminded him.

Logan saw the curiosity in his father's eyes turn into blatant disapproval. "Emma hired you," he said. "But I recall having a conversation with you about fraternizing with the guests."

"Yes, we did."

"I don't have to ask what you're doing here now," he said with scorn.

Logan was tempted to jump in and protect her, but he sensed if he violated her sense of confidence, she'd never forgive him. Hell, he was lucky if she'd talk to him again either way.

Her gaze never wavered from his father's. To Catherine's credit, considering she wore nothing but his oxford shirt, she held her own with the man who intimidated even those who knew him best.

"No, you don't. But since I'm not on your payroll anymore, there's really not much you can say. But I would like to tell you one thing before I go."

"Catherine, you don't have to put up with this in my house."

"No, I don't." She smiled at him, but there was no joy in the gesture. "Just call this my parting gift." She turned back to the judge. "The more you try to control the people you love, the farther away they'll run." Cat cleared her throat. "Sir."

Before his father could register her words, she ducked past him. By the time he'd begun to react, Cat had hit the open button on the remote control and ducked safely inside the Jeep.

Pride along with regret swelled inside him as Logan watched the media frenzy that followed her departure. Controlling his anger at his father wasn't easy and he took a minute to center himself.

"Luck," the judge muttered. "I remember that name. Big news around every state courthouse. She's got spunk and attitude. Not surprising given her roots, but admirable just the same." He met Logan's gaze. "Now would you care to tell me what's going on between the two of you? And how you intend to explain it to the press?"

Anger seethed beneath the surface but Logan took his lead from Cat. He had to maintain control. Judge Montgomery never lost his cool. Determination and an air of authority would get Logan further than losing his temper, something he'd learned as a child. The best way to reach him was to meet him on a level playing field. Humor and dry sarcasm wasn't going to cut it anymore. The plain, honest facts were.

On his own schedule, Logan turned to his father. "I have nothing to explain to the press. Or to you.

I don't know what it's going to take to convince you that I call the shots in my life. And in my house." He drew a deep breath. "And I resent like hell the way you spoke to the woman I love."

The judge shook his head. "I don't understand you, son. You're young and I can see her appeal, much as I hate to admit it. But you don't throw away your life for love. It doesn't exist. An equal partnership does. And that's what a political man needs. A woman capable of looking good and standing by her man. No scandals involved."

Logan raised an eyebrow. "I'm not a political man. I never will be. Do you hear what I'm saying? You can't keep circling the issue. I'm not running for mayor. And I'm not going to take a job at a high-powered firm, or move into a luxury building or, worse, back into the mansion."

His father let out a long-suffering sigh. "You choose to live in this...shack. Your mother and I have accepted it. Obviously we have no choice. But just because you live below your means doesn't mean you have to consort with lower-class women, too."

Now he'd gone too far. Logan clenched his fists, unwilling to listen to his father insult a woman he didn't know. *His* woman, Logan thought, and it was time the judge understood that.

"Listen to me, because I'm only going to say this once. You will not insult the woman I plan to marry. Do you understand? She's going to be your daughter-in-law. Accept her or walk out of my life, because, on that score, there's no compromise." Logan's head throbbed in time to his words.

For all their posturing and arguing, there'd never been a time when he'd completely removed himself from his family. Physically, yes, he'd moved out. Mentally he was on his own. But emotionally, he'd clung to the hope that one day he'd have the solid family he'd always wanted.

His father grew pale beneath his golfing tan. He grabbed for the wall behind him for support and Logan reached for his father. "Dad?" He'd never had cause to question his father's health before and fear paralleled his anger.

"Don't be ridiculous." His father regained his composure quickly, as well as his angry pallor. "The woman ingratiated herself with a senile old woman so she could end up exactly where she is now. In your bed."

Disappointment and regret lanced through Logan. His father would never see the truth any more than he would accept what was important in life. "Goodbye, Dad."

"Son, consider your future. You don't have to ruin your life just to thwart me. *Think*. Family unity is important. I know that. Why do you think I found a way to use your...lifestyle to our advantage? This photo opportunity would have set you up as the Montgomery who relates to the common man. As usual, you destroyed my efforts. But I tried. You need to do the same."

Logan shook his head. "If family unity is so important to you, *you* do the thinking. Think about everything I said here today because I meant it. Give up the need to control me and accept my life. Accept Catherine."

The judge grunted. "Her appeal will wear thin," he said, but for the first time, he didn't sound so certain.

"Never."

"You have too much of your grandmother in you," he muttered. "You realize you have the press waiting. What do you intend to tell them?"

"The truth."

Without another word, Edgar walked out the door.

Logan shook his head. He wished things could be different, but he couldn't dwell on it now. He had a life to reclaim as his own. By the time he was through, who Logan Montgomery was and where he was headed would be clear to everyone.

Including Catherine.

CHAPTER ELEVEN

CATHERINE'S HEAD HURT and she could say for certain it was from stress. Along with her assistants, she'd spent the afternoon creating centerpieces for the next day's party. The small studio she and Kayla had rented for Pot Luck's place of business was filled to bursting. All that work should have left her spent, especially since she'd gotten little sleep the night before.

Her body still tingled in the places Logan had touched. She shivered at the memory, then decided she obviously wasn't exhausted enough if she had the ability to think about, let alone react to, the thought of making love with Logan.

Determined to forget, Catherine retrieved the flour and then pulled the milk and eggs out of the refrigerator. Sugar and water came next. After this morning's nightmare with the press, she was so worked up, she would probably end up with enough food to feed the entire apartment building. She'd settle for feeding Nick and his fiancée who lived across the hall.

She began mixing the ingredients with a wire whisk and a harder hand than necessary. Never mind that Nick's crepes could put hers to shame, enthusiasm and surplus energy had to count for something.

The ring of the telephone didn't startle her. She'd been logging in calls every thirty minutes for the better part of the evening. Logan had called five times so far, according to the tally on the machine. She'd listened to his concerned message once. After that she'd turned the sound all the way down. She didn't want to speak to Logan and she wasn't ready to hear his voice.

Not until the embarrassment faded. Not until she could understand how a family could set each other up and not care about the outcome. She and Logan had never seriously discussed the future, but even if they had, Catherine didn't know if she could accept living in a fishbowl, never certain when the next incident would spring up to humiliate her. The only positive thing about today was her confrontation with Judge Montgomery. At least she'd left him feeling like his equal, not just the hired help he'd demeaned at the party last week.

She continued mixing the batter, slowly adding more milk. She already had the fresh blueberry sauce sitting in a bowl beside the cooktop, ready to go. She wiped her itchy nose with the back of her hand and wondered what her mama would say if she knew Catherine had willingly walked away from the man she loved. *You'd be a fool to let that man go, Catherine Ann.*

Of course, Mama had lived and died by that particular axiom, Catherine thought. And she refused to become a replica of her mother, pretending to be better than she was, and pining for a man she couldn't have. Or in this case, *shouldn't* have. It all amounted to the same thing. Logan Montgomery meant pain and heartache.

The sound of the doorbell came as a welcome reprieve from being alone with her thoughts. She swung the door open wide. "Your stomach is huge, Nick. I said I'd call when the crepes were…" Her voice trailed off as she caught sight of her visitor. "Logan."

"Obviously you were expecting someone else. Sorry to disappoint you."

He could never disappoint her. Even with two days' razor stubble and a weariness etched into his eyes she'd never seen before, he was still the answer to her every dream. Too bad she'd been brought crashing into reality, or she'd be more receptive to the fantasy. "What can I do for you?" she asked.

He propped one arm on the door frame. "Let me in, for starters."

She drew a deep breath, unsure if she wanted him to enter. At least in her apartment, there were no memories of him besides the ones she conjured in her head.

"You have my car so I had to pay for a cab ride out here. You wouldn't turn away a poor working man, now would you?" he asked, a charming but wary grin on his face.

Nick would have driven his car back tomorrow, but she doubted Logan wanted to hear Nick's name mentioned right now. She also doubted he'd accept his car keys at the door and be on his way. Her best bet was to stay composed and detached. Get him in and out—of her apartment as well as her life—no matter how much the thought hurt. "Come on in."

She stepped aside and as he passed her, she caught a whiff of his distinctive scent and her knees nearly buckled under her. So much for remaining detached. She wondered if she could pull off the composed and aloof routine. She doubted it.

He walked into her small living area and

glanced around at her furniture. Dressed in a black polo shirt and denim jeans, he looked at home in her cozy apartment. And that was the last thing she wanted him to be.

He appraised the room from top to bottom before focusing his attention on her living room carpet, one of her favorite furnishings. He raised an eyebrow at the leopard-patterned area rug covering the hardwood floor. No way he'd understand her love of animal prints.

"It'd go well in the cottage," he said.

Her heart nearly stopped beating. "What do you want from me? Don't you think today's proven just how impossible this is?" She gestured back and forth between the two of them, keeping a physical distance.

He closed that fast and she found herself surrounded by his masculine presence. Reaching out, his finger brushed at her nose. "Flour?" he asked.

She nodded, trying not to acknowledge how much that simple gesture affected her. Self-conscious now, she rubbed her nose with the back of her hand. "I'm making crepes."

"Sounds delicious." His stomach rumbled and she laughed.

"Sounds more like you're hungry," she said.

He grinned. "So feed me."

Without another word, she walked over to the pass-through area between her walk-in kitchen and the living room. "I hope you're not starving because I don't have much," she warned him. She was due for a supermarket run. Her cupboards were almost bare except for junk food and the standard things she kept for elaborate baking.

"Whatever you've got is okay by me." He made himself at home, sitting on one of her bar stools that doubled as her kitchen chairs.

She sighed and decided junk food would do just fine. She dug into her cabinets, grabbed her only choice and headed back to Logan. "Here you go, eat up." She tossed a box of Cracker Jacks at him.

He shrugged. "Love this stuff."

"Figures," she muttered aloud.

He tore into the box and held it toward her. "Want some?"

She shook her head. "No, thank you."

"Then don't let me keep you." He popped a caramel piece of corn into his mouth, then gestured toward her baking ingredients. "I'd love to watch."

She sighed and glanced at the batter, which still needed thinning.

"You shouldn't have had to go through what happened this morning," he said.

The sudden change of subject caught her off guard. She glanced at his serious expression, not sure what to say in return.

"I don't know if the picture will hit the paper or not," he said, when she remained silent.

"What you can't control, you ignore." Or tried to. She'd spent the afternoon trying to come to terms with the fact that she'd be plastered all over some gossip section of a local paper. "Any chance they'll bury it on the back page?" she asked.

"Doubtful. And I wish it hadn't happened."

She met his gaze. "Maybe so, but did it accomplish your goal?" she asked.

He raised an eyebrow. "You can't believe I had anything to do with that press conference."

She shook her head. If there was anything in life she was certain of, it was Logan's integrity. "Of course not." She wrapped her hand tight around the whisk. The edges of metal bit into her skin. "But can you deny that getting caught half-naked with the woman of the day will help derail your father's campaign?"

She held her breath, waiting for his answer. As if whatever he said would change what had happened, what was or wasn't meant to be.

"I wish I could."

And she wished he'd denied that she was his woman of the moment and felt let down that he hadn't. What a bundle of contradictions she'd become, Catherine thought. Pushing him away with one breath, wishing he'd come back with the next. Never in her life had she been at such loose ends, so confused over her feelings.

No, that was wrong, she amended. She was quite certain of her feelings. She loved a man she couldn't have.

"So how did your father take the news that there wouldn't be a run for mayor?" she asked.

No way Logan would repeat the judge's tirade. Logan grunted. "Not well."

He dug farther into the coated candy. "As usual, I disappointed him." And as usual, Logan felt the same swell of disappointment in his father, because they couldn't find any common ground and, this time, the rift would be permanent.

"I'm sorry." She'd braced her hands against the counter and studied him. "Will he get over it?" she asked.

Logan shrugged. "I really couldn't tell you."

"But you want him to, don't you? You'd like to be some sort of family, wouldn't you?"

"Not if the judge is going to act like a pompous, overbearing…"

"No cursing in my kitchen," she said, before he could get his next words out.

He laughed. "You know me too well. But yes, if there was a way to come to an understanding without compromising my life, I'd take it."

"Then try with your mother. You never know."

Logan nodded slowly. Catherine was right. He hadn't exhausted every avenue toward peace. When his father had turned pale and grabbed for the wall, Logan realized how badly he'd wanted the judge to come around. The idea of losing him permanently had frightened him. But the older man had recovered quickly, both his pallor and his temper.

He chewed on a bite of candy. Catherine was busy stirring and ignoring him. He dug into the box once more. This time he came up with the prize, a green plastic ring. Knowing all a ring could symbolize, Logan was amazed. Sometimes fate did smile.

Until he'd told his father he intended to marry Catherine, he hadn't realized that was exactly what he planned. In his gut he'd known it all along. Not that she'd take well to the idea. Not yet. She needed time, which was fine since it would give him more time to get to know her as well.

Without warning, Catherine reached through the pass-through and touched his arm. Her soft gaze settled on his. "Family's family. Don't you think your mother would want to help you and your father reach a compromise?"

After the way his father had treated her, he was amazed she could still push for him. But she had no father to speak of and less family than he did. She obviously felt the loss and wanted to prevent him from suffering the same emptiness. Emptiness he wanted to fill for her.

And he would, his family be damned.

He discreetly shoved the prize into his front pants pocket. "I'll think about everything you said. But unless he stops interfering in my life, there can't be any compromise. Now, can we stop talking about a mayoral race that isn't happening?"

She shook her head. "I thought we were talking about your need for family."

He met her gaze and his mouth twisted into a smile. "I guess we were." He propped his elbows on the bleached wood counter. "So let's talk about us."

Her reluctant grin pleased him. "You never give up, do you?" she asked.

"Nope." And he wouldn't. Not until she looked at him with trust and love shining in those green eyes.

He'd put the old man in his place. Regaining Catherine's trust couldn't be nearly as tough—as long as no other outside forces interfered again.

CATHERINE GLANCED AT Logan and shook her head. It wasn't fair, that charm and charisma he possessed. He could twist her around his finger so easily. Too easily, she thought with chagrin. She spun the whisk back and forth between her palms.

"So tell me why you're so afraid to let yourself go, Cat."

She was suddenly grateful she had something to do with her hands and began beating the mixture in the bowl without meeting his gaze. "Because I can't. Did I tell you my father ran out on my mother?" she asked, unsure why she was revealing such personal information, why she'd chosen this particular time.

She'd never discussed her childhood with anyone but Kayla. Yet with Logan it seemed right.

He leaned forward in his seat. "You alluded to it."

"Well, he took off on her and two kids."

"And you think any guy you'll get involved with will do the same?"

She shook her head. "It's not that. But life comes with obstacles. It doesn't matter if you're poor and have a hard time paying the bills, or the happiest couple with everything in common, life will throw you a curve."

She shrugged, finding the explanation more difficult than she thought. She took some time to compose her thoughts and he seemed to understand, granting her the silence she needed. Another special thing about Logan was his ability to listen and the comfortable silences they were able to fall into together.

She shook her head. She was supposed to be explaining their obstacles not finding things they had in common. "If you're different people to start with, or have problems on the horizon, you've already got the deck stacked against you." She let out a heartfelt sigh. "*We* have the deck stacked against us."

On the surface, Logan supposed her explanation made sense. To her at least.

He didn't agree. They had more in common than she wanted to admit, and few problems on the horizon that he could see. He'd already taken care of the biggest one. If his father had to choose between his beliefs and his son, he'd choose his pompous ideals. It hurt, but Logan had already accepted that reality many times in the past.

So now his family didn't stand in their way. Nothing did but Catherine herself. She had her reasoning all twisted around so that she believed she had logic on her side. But the core of her fear lay in being abandoned. And because of their differences, she probably thought the risk of him leaving her was too high for her to take a chance on.

He met her green-eyed gaze and held it fast. "The deck's only stacked against us if you choose to believe it is."

"Are we back to dreams again?"

He shook his head. "We're back to reality. To the fact that, yes, life can intrude on the best of couples. But if they work hard enough, if they stick together, they get through it together."

He wondered if she was really listening and realized her eyes remained steady on his. They were suspiciously damp. She was more than paying attention. She was digesting his words. He'd give her a few minutes in peaceful silence to take his words to heart.

Her fingers toyed with a tiny pendant at the end of a gold chain, drawing his attention to the pale skin visible between the open collar of the blouse she wore rolled up at the sleeves. The gap in the cleavage wasn't something he could ignore, though he'd been trying for the past half hour.

What he felt for Catherine was greater than lust, even if his growing erection and overwhelming desire to make love to her on the flour-coated kitchen counter threatened to make that statement a lie. And he intended to prove it to her.

Before he acted on need and not common sense, Logan rose to his feet. He had to get the hell out of here and home to an ice-cold shower. He doubted even the hour ride back to the beach would cool his desire.

He said what he'd come to say. He'd leave her alone with her thoughts and trust she'd come to have faith in him.

"You're leaving?" Her voice broke the silence.

"I'd better. You have to work in the morning."

She nodded, then headed out of the kitchen. She grabbed his keys from a side table and met him on his walk to the door. "Logan, you've been…"

"Don't say it."

She tipped her head to the side. "Why not?" she asked. Her nose crinkled in confusion. "You have no idea what I was about to say."

"Right. And I'd like to leave it that way."

Before she tried for goodbye, see you sometime, or some other lame line he didn't want to hear. He dug his hands into his front jeans pocket. "But I do want to give you something before I go."

She shook her head. "I can't take anything from you."

He grinned. "Sure you can." He dug into his pocket, then opened his hand, palm up and revealed the plastic ring with a shimmering sticker on the top. He couldn't have planned it better if he'd tried.

Jewels and money would turn Catherine off. He had a hunch this small gesture would mean much more.

"What's that?" Even as she asked, her lips turned upward in a smile and it took all his self-control not to kiss her senseless.

"My ring," he said and grinned. "Want to go steady?"

If Catherine's heart hadn't already belonged to Logan Montgomery, it would now. She looked down at the plastic ring in his hand. Such a small token—from a candy box, no less. How could it mean so much?

She picked up the plastic bauble from his hand. It wasn't gold or diamonds or some expensive gesture to win her over. It was a gift from his heart.

How could she not accept it? How could she deny her own heart any longer, let alone his?

Catherine slipped the ring onto the third finger on her right hand.

His gaze followed the movement. "I'll be calling you," he said in a husky voice. "Later tonight."

Her stomach coiled into a tight knot. "What if I said don't go?" She reached out for his hand, locking their fingers together.

His touch was hot, his gaze hotter. "Then I'd ask if you were sure."

Sure she wanted to be with him? Without a doubt. Sure she was doing the right thing? Well, maybe it was time to take that leap of faith. "I'm sure."

He cupped her cheeks in his hand and lowered his head, meeting her lips with his. The warmth and tenderness in his touch caused a spiraling heat and a tidal wave of emotion to surge through her. Desire and the urge to have him inside her rose as fast as her remaining doubts fled.

When she reached for the button on his jeans, he unlocked their other hands and stopped her. "I didn't come here for this."

If his breathing hadn't been ragged and his expression tortured—if she didn't feel the hard, heavy press of his erection where their bodies met—she might have felt embarrassed or vulnerable. But Logan obviously wasn't saying he didn't want her.

"Are you afraid you'll take advantage of me? I know what I want," she said quietly. "I want *you*." Her rapidly beating heart and the sudden liquid rush of desire attested to that.

"No more than I want you."

"Then there's no problem."

He groaned and touched his forehead to hers. "Desire's never been a problem between us. Sex has never been the issue."

Afraid she knew where this was leading, Catherine merely sighed. The man could probably see inside her soul. She had no doubt her feelings were mirrored in her face. There was little she could hide from him anymore, and even less she wanted to. She waited for him to continue.

"We could make love now and there'd still be your fears to deal with in the morning. You admitted as much tonight."

"Is that what we'd be doing? Making love?" She hated the raw tone in her voice.

With that one question, she'd not only bared

her soul, but her heart. By avoiding the issue of her fears, she'd set them squarely between them. She'd never trusted anyone not to trample her heart before, and by doing so now, she'd given Logan power that was frightening.

He caressed her cheek with his thumb. "We've never done anything *but* make love, Cat."

Her breath caught in her throat as emotion warred with sexual need. Her heart felt full to bursting. So did her body, because a throbbing, aching need had overtaken it.

"But we aren't going to do it tonight."

Despite her body's protest to his words, she smiled. "You're a gentleman, Logan Montgomery."

"A damned uncomfortable one," he muttered and she couldn't help but laugh. "What can I say? My grandmother raised me right." He grinned, but she saw the same strain in his expression she felt herself.

"Yes, she did." Catherine twisted the plastic ring on her finger.

"Did you ever go steady before?"

"Not since high school." And not all that often, she realized, thinking back to those days. She hadn't wanted anyone to get that close, to see where and how her family lived.

"What do you remember most? And I'm not talking about making out in the back seat of some guy's car."

She raised an eyebrow. "Logan Montgomery threatened by some football jock who's probably balding and has a beer belly by now?" She patted her stomach and laughed.

"I don't like the thought of anyone's hands on you—" he paused a beat "—except mine."

She liked the possessiveness in his voice, but that darned honesty got in the way. "Actually I don't remember much," she admitted. "There really wasn't anyone who lasted longer than a day or two." When she was in her teens, she wasn't ready for a steady boyfriend. By the time she'd hit her twenties, she'd developed the ability to date and remain detached. She'd had a couple of intimate relationships but none that had truly touched her heart.

He squeezed her hand. "Then let me be the first to introduce you to the idea." The laughter and fun dancing in his dark eyes were contagious.

"I'm listening."

CHAPTER TWELVE

LOGAN TOOK HER HAND and led her back through the apartment until they reached the soft, black, faux leather couch. Pulling her down beside him, he drew her close. "Going steady involves a lot of drive-through fast-food restaurants, for one thing." His hands eased under her shirt until his palms rested, warm and strong, against her skin.

Her heart started beating heavily again and she licked her dry lips. "What else?"

"Parking on a deserted road." His hands inched upward until they settled just below her breasts.

Her skin tingled where he touched and her stomach clenched with an aching need.

"No bra again, Cat." He made a *tsk-tsking* sound.

"I wasn't expecting…" His fingertips swiped at her nipple and she sucked in a startled gasp. Fiery darts of pleasure pricked at her nerve endings. "Company," she somehow choked out.

"I thought we weren't going to do this." Not that she wanted to discourage him. Just the opposite. So she leaned back, settling herself between his legs and giving his hands better access to her chest.

He nuzzled her neck with his lips. His hot moist breath tickled her sensitive skin and his hands lingered, as he cupped her breasts in his hands. "I see I have a lot to teach you," he murmured in her ear.

Full and heavy, she felt the weight of her breasts settle into his palms. "Parking involves forbidden desire. I want you, you want me...but we know it's too soon." He continued to explain. All the while his thumbs wreaked havoc on her senses by rolling and pulling her nipples into tight peaks, and his lips traveled a moist path up her neck.

She sighed aloud, half hoping he'd understand what she needed, even if she wasn't sure herself.

"When you're parking, you can do anything you want." He grasped her earlobe between his teeth and pulled. The stinging sensation traveled straight downward and she clenched her thighs together tight. But the empty, longing sensation remained.

"Anything?" she asked. Her need was so great she'd do anything to alleviate the pulsing, pounding desire. Waves of longing rolled over her, intense and strong.

"Almost anything," he replied. Without warning, he turned her around, caught her beneath him on the couch. His arms bracketed her, and he eased himself down until he lay on top of her, chest to chest. His erection pressed strongly against her, ready and wanting just like she was.

"I think I like this parking business," she managed to say through labored breaths.

He laughed. "Done like this, I have to agree. It's a lot more comfortable on a full-length couch in an air-conditioned apartment. But I'd be happy anywhere, as long as I was with you." His hips jerked against hers.

His swollen desire pushed insistently against her and moist liquid trickled between her legs. She leaned her head back and moaned with pleasure.

Without warning, he began a grinding motion, a circular press of his hips, that pushed her into the couch and ground his hard erection into her. "Now this is what parking's all about," he whispered in her ear.

The waves came fast and furious, bringing her closer and closer to the edge. "Logan…"

"Go with it, sweetheart."

"But you're not, we're not…"

He groaned, pumping his body into hers. "Yes, Cat, we are." He let out a harsh breath.

Minutes later, still wrapped in his arms, Catherine nuzzled her cheek into his. This was as close to perfect as life could get. If she was in heaven, she never wanted to wake up.

And if life never intruded again, she never would.

SWEET SIXTEEN, Catherine thought as she placed the balloon-laden centerpiece on the last table. She stepped back to admire her handiwork. The pink and white balloons intermingled with gold Mylar and red roses were a testament to the young girl's youthful dreams—and Catherine thought, the love of her parents. The soon-to-be sixteen-year-old was very lucky.

She looked around the room once more, and ascertaining the tables were complete and the party favors were in the corner, she headed out. The restaurant was handling the catering. All Pot Luck had been hired for were decorations. Her job here was done.

In the week since the Montgomery party, Catherine had received a flurry of phone calls and had set up appointments with many of Hampshire's residents who had been at the Montgomery Garden Gala. Although Pot Luck had catered a classy affair, Catherine knew she had Emma to thank for the ensuing referrals. But that had been before her run-in with Judge Montgomery. She couldn't imagine what the fallout from that episode would be.

Nor, she realized, did she care. She and Kayla had built a catering business in one short year. They'd been doing fine before they'd known the name Montgomery and they'd do fine after. Business-wise, Catherine was happy with her life and she'd survive without Montgomery referrals, if need be.

But she wouldn't survive without Logan. Her heart knew it as well as her mind. The question remained: What did she intend to do about it?

When she hit the top of the stairs, exhaustion overtook her. Her body still tingled from the pleasure Logan had given her last night and her mind soared with possibilities. The front of the restaurant was comprised of a waiting area and a bar. The stools looked cushioned and comfortable and she didn't think anyone would mind if she grabbed one and rested before making the half hour drive back to Boston.

"Drink?" The bartender who'd been wiping down glasses paused in front of her.

Catherine shook her head.

"Come on, I saw you unload that van of balloons yourself. Have a drink. It's on the house."

Catherine smiled. "How can I refuse an offer like that? Club soda with a twist of lime."

"You got it." He flipped on the television sitting high above the bar. "My girlfriend does a local entertainment show at noon."

"Mmm. Good for her."

"Yeah. She's hoping the bigger networks will pick her up one day. For now she's happy doing weekends on the local station. There she is now." With a flip of the remote he raised the volume.

Except for the trickle of people beginning to flow to the party downstairs, no other patrons were in the bar. Catherine found it easy to relax and focus on the television show. "She's got poise," Catherine murmured, glancing at the woman on the screen.

The bartender nodded. "Sure does. I just hope she gets the break she deserves."

Catherine nodded. She blinked and the next thing she saw was Logan's beachfront cottage. Warning bells and an unwelcome sense of foreboding sent her apprehension soaring. "Make it louder, please."

"See? She's even won you over."

Catherine ignored him, focusing on the screen. The anchorwoman's voice-over did little to calm the churning in Catherine's stomach. This was not good. She'd avoided picking up today's paper, afraid of what she'd see. Although she knew she couldn't avoid the headlines forever, she'd wanted to bask in the memories of last night for as long as possible. She also hadn't expected television coverage of Judge Montgomery's arranged event.

Just what do you think a press conference entails, Catherine? She shook her head and concentrated on the cultured, feminine voice. "Hampshire's boy wonder, Logan Montgomery, firmly dispelled any rumors of an impending run for mayor. Despite Judge Montgomery's posturing and claims to the contrary, the younger Montgomery insists he will *not* be running for office."

Catherine smiled. At least Logan had swayed the media to see things his way. The screen went from the beautiful young anchor to Logan, standing in his standard jeans and pullover, his cottage in the background. He looked sexily disheveled and Catherine knew she had helped cause that rumpled look before they'd been caught by the photographers.

Logan's voice cut into her thoughts. "...and while I appreciate the confidence of the judge and other supporters, running for mayor is not in my plans."

"And what would those plans be, Mr. Montgomery?" a reporter's voice sounded.

"After my stay at the public defender's office, I intend to open my own practice where clients will be offered affordable representation."

Catherine couldn't help but notice his class and poise. If he'd chosen to run for mayor, he'd make a formidable opponent. Composed and sure of himself, it would take an incredible opposing candidate to beat his charismatic charm. She also noticed his father was not by his side during this speech.

Her heart squeezed at the thought of him standing up to the judge and coming out on top, but still alone. She wondered what had transpired between the two men after her abrupt departure. Logan had been deliberately vague on the subject. She could only imagine his father's displeasure at finding them together. Not that he'd realized right away who she was.

"Every generation of Montgomerys has either sat on the bench or held public office, conquered the world by leaps and bounds. Doesn't it bother you to break with tradition?" the reporter asked.

"Not at all." Logan looked straight into the camera. "I'd rather conquer the world *one* person at a time."

Catherine's stomach curled into a delicious knot. With his emphasis on the word one, and the intense, focused look in his eyes, he might as well have been gazing into *her* eyes and promising *her* his undying devotion.

They'd said as much with their bodies last night. The unspoken words meant little when the actions were there. For the first time today she realized he'd managed to convince her that different backgrounds didn't matter as much as she thought.

Without warning, the camera panned back and the anchorwoman's serious face replaced Logan's smile. "Mr. Montgomery's pullback from a speculated run for office couldn't have come at a more convenient time. Minutes before the scheduled press conference, this picture was taken of Mr. Montgomery in a *compromising* position."

Catherine's nightmare flashed on the television screen for the world to see. Well, for all of Boston to see since this was a local station, but that didn't ease the sudden pain in her chest. There she was, Logan's shirt pulled up to her thighs, his arms wrapped around her waist and his cutoff shorts, his only clothing, hidden by their entangled position.

"Hey, isn't that—"

"Me," she said, cutting the bartender off, then she turned her attention back to the screen.

"Logan Montgomery's companion is Catherine Luck, co-owner, with her sister, Kayla Luck, of a local catering and party company, whimsically named Pot Luck."

"No publicity is bad publicity," Catherine muttered aloud. She held her head in her hands and continued to watch her life be made fodder for gossip, speculation and ridicule, just as she'd feared.

She wasn't immune to the embarrassment. Neither, Catherine suspected, was her pregnant and emotionally vulnerable sister.

"The Luck sisters are best known for the scandal involving an inherited business, a charm school for men, that turned out to be a front for a prostitution ring with ties to organized crime..."

Good God, what would they drag up next?

"...and, with her working-class background Catherine Luck is not the woman one would expect to see Logan Montgomery consorting with. But a romp on the beach is far different from a lifetime…"

Entertainment show? More like gossip and tabloid exploitation, she thought with disgust. She didn't have to take any more. "Shut it off. Please."

The bartender glanced from Catherine's face to his girlfriend on the screen. He turned off the television.

Catherine tried to breathe but her heart was beating so rapidly she thought her chest might explode. Thinking was near impossible, but she forced herself to concentrate and her first coherent thought was of Kayla. Bed rest and a high-risk pregnancy. Catherine had to check on her sister.

If she'd seen the news, Catherine had to minimize the damage. If Kayla had missed the local broadcast, then Catherine wanted to be the person to break the newest scandal to her sister. And to Kane. At the thought of the overprotective cop, Catherine winced.

She grabbed her purse and bolted outside. Until she'd made sure Kayla was okay, Catherine couldn't think of the ramifications to herself. But she'd have to, and soon, she thought, fingering the plastic ring on her finger.

Not to mention the ramifications to her relationship with Logan.

"SHE'S NOT ANSWERING the phone but I'd lay odds she's there." Logan muttered a frustrated curse.

"I don't like this." Emma paced the linoleum floor of his office. She'd arrived soon after him, shared coffee and commiserated over his stint on the news. With his friends and colleagues ribbing him, he appreciated her support.

The sun shone brightly through the battered blinds but Logan barely felt the heat. "I don't like it, either," he muttered.

"Call her again."

"I've been calling on the hour since last night."

Catherine hadn't answered the phone. She hadn't returned his calls. And he didn't think she was coincidentally busy or out of touch.

His once solitary life had become a recipe for disaster. Catherine, the one woman he'd ever fallen for, was the one woman who shouldn't be subjected to the indignities of the press. The photo of Logan and Catherine on the beach had passed from newspaper to newspaper, tabloid to tabloid, and from local news to local gossip shows—all in record time. Logan hadn't realized the public had such a raging interest in his sex life. It would almost be funny if the consequences weren't so dire.

He grabbed for the phone and punched in her number once more.

"Is she in labor?" To his shock, Catherine's concerned voice answered after the first ring.

"Cat?"

"Logan."

"You were expecting Kane," he said. It wasn't a hard guess.

"Yes."

He expected a strained silence to follow, but she continued to speak instead. "To be honest, now's not a good time."

Not that he liked what she had to say. "Gossip stinks, Cat, but it has nothing to do with us."

He heard a distinctive beep and knew she'd gotten another call on the line. He muttered a curse.

"What'd she say?" Emma asked, leaning too close to the receiver.

He shooed her away and she went gracefully, seating herself in the old chair across from his desk. One good thing that had come out of this fiasco was Emma's new-found grace, dignity and respect for his private life.

"I've got to go," Catherine said.

"Take the call and come back to me. I'll hang on." He knew how important her sister was in her life. Although Logan wouldn't stand in the way of her obvious fear and concern, he wouldn't cut her loose without a fight, either.

"I can't think about myself now."

The question was, would she think about them later or would she use this time to retreat further away? He drew a deep breath, then another, ignoring his hovering grandmother.

He had no choice but to grab opportunity when he had the chance. "Then think about this. I love you."

Her soft gasp of shock was cut off by the damned insistent call-waiting. "I can't do this now. I'm sorry. Goodbye, Logan."

"Just think about it, Cat."

"I can't." The phone intruded again. "I'm hanging up now," she said before severing the connection.

He snorted in frustration at her use of Emma's tactic and hung up the phone, his stomach in twisted knots.

"You are going after her, aren't you? Because I have an idea. We can…"

"Forget it, Gran. I'll handle this myself."

"Fine, leave an old lady out of the fun. Deny

me my enjoyment in life." She let out a long-suf-fering sigh.

He rolled his eyes. "You'll survive."

"Well then, I have a car waiting for me outside."

"I'll walk you to the elevator," Logan said.

"No need. I'd like to hang by the water cooler a while first."

Logan grinned. "I do love you, Gran."

Emma smiled. "I love you, too. And so does Catherine." His grandmother kissed his cheek. "Even if she didn't say it back."

He shook his head. "You're too perceptive, smart and nosy for my own good."

"Ah, but I spice up your life."

"That you do."

He watched her regal retreat and heard her voice as she mingled with the office staff. Knowing she was occupied not meddling in his life gave him time to think about Cat.

Then think about this. I love you, he'd told her. Logan didn't mind giving her his heart, but if she wanted to accept it, she was going to have to come to him.

KAYLA AND KANE had a baby boy. Catherine stretched her feet out in front of her on the plasticlike couch in the hospital waiting room. She hung her head backward, breathing deeply for the first time in what felt like hours.

Her sister had a family of her own now. One that didn't include her. Oh, they'd never exclude her, and she planned to be the best aunt in the universe to that child, but she wasn't a part of their immediate family.

Not in the ways that counted. Why did that bother her so much? When had she begun wanting more out of a life she'd thought made her happy?

When she'd met Logan. He'd dredged up her old class-difference insecurities, then set out to overcome them. To make her believe she could have everything in life, even a man from a wealthy family.

She sat up in her seat, realizing she was up to the challenge. The entertainment show, and she used that term loosely, had opened her eyes to a lot of things. So had the birth of this baby.

A new life meant new possibilities. New directions. Catherine could learn from that. She wasn't defined by her past. So she'd come from a poor background. She'd gotten beyond it. The judge would have to as well, because Catherine wasn't going anywhere.

She wanted all the things in life her sister had

found and she was determined to get them. Her heart still fluttered when she remembered his unexpected words.

I love you.

Well, she loved him too and she was darn well going to show him.

"...THE CHARGES AGAINST the defendant are dismissed. Court is adjourned." The judge banged his gavel and strode from the room. After a brief handshake with his ecstatic client, Logan heaved a groan of relief. The case from hell was over.

He tossed his pad, pen and other things into his briefcase, grateful it was only Tuesday and he was looking forward to a quiet end of the week. Not surprisingly, his thoughts turned to Catherine. He hadn't heard from her. Not one word.

Logan was as understanding as the next guy, but he'd discovered something about himself. His desire to be her lapdog only went so far. He'd extended himself as much as he could without compromising his integrity.

I love you weren't words he said idly or to every woman he'd dated. In fact, he'd never said them before. And he wouldn't be saying them again, unless she decided to get in touch with him.

But that didn't stop his concern, and he'd called Kane yesterday to check on Catherine's sister and had sent a bundle of balloons to celebrate the birth of their baby.

"Mr. Montgomery."

Logan turned to face the bailiff who ran the courtroom. "How's it going, Stan?"

"Fine. I have a message for you." The burly man passed Logan a white, sealed envelope.

He loosened his tie and examined the generic envelope. "From whom?"

"Pretty lady. Blond. Five foot three or so... Smelled like Opium," he said, naming a popular feminine fragrance.

Logan grinned. "Ever think of going into detective work? You've got a hell of a memory."

"Nah. She's just too much to forget. I've gotta get home or the wife'll kill me. Have a good one, Montgomery."

"You, too, Stan."

Curious now, Logan opened the envelope. As he pulled out the folded sheet inside, a sprinkling of what looked like confetti fell to the floor at his feet. He unfolded the sheet and read aloud. *"Come Home."*

Logan's heart sprung into action, beating too hard and too fast—as if it had been lying dormant, waiting for Catherine's return. He glanced toward the doorway, but the courtroom was empty.

Still, he understood the message. She'd put aside her doubts and her fears. She was ready to place her faith in the unknown. He knew what that leap of faith cost her. He intended to make sure she never regretted it.

He grabbed his briefcase and headed out the door into the dwindling heat of the day.

What was it he'd said the first time he'd taken her to the beach house? *It's humble but it's home.* She'd glanced around the run-down cottage, the idea of which had sent other women running, and greeted him with an approving gleam in her green eyes. *Home. It is that,* she'd murmured.

He'd probably fallen in love then and there.

Logan slid into the Jeep and turned the ignition. What felt like hours but could only have been twenty minutes later, he finally walked up to his cottage. The Pot Luck company van sat parked in the driveway.

He turned the knob. Not surprisingly, the door was open. After days of uncertainty, the adrenaline rush felt damn good. Knowing she was inside, but not knowing exactly what awaited him left him breathless with anticipation.

He *wanted* her and she was here. He stepped inside and shut the door. Placing his briefcase on the floor, he glanced around. The spring weather was still cool and a fire crackled in the hearth, the scent of fresh-burning wood enveloping him.

"Cat?" he called out, but she didn't answer, so he walked in farther, pausing in the kitchen. Though she wasn't inside, she'd made her presence known. His old table had been transformed.

A beige tablecloth draped his wooden table, hiding the old scars and nicks. Candles burned in holders he'd never seen before and a bouquet of spring flowers sat low in the center. A heavenly smell hit his nostrils and he realized she'd been cooking.

Wondering what else she'd been doing, he backed out of the dimly lit kitchen and headed for the bedroom. He didn't need a map to guide him to a room he'd been in dozens of times before. But Catherine had been thoughtful, leaving him a trail to follow.

A sexy, seductive trail, he thought, as he bent down and picked up the first article of clothing at the end of the hall. Leopard sandals dangled from his fingertips. Need kicked in, intense and strong.

He took a step farther and retrieved a black skirt. Another step and he'd reached the bedroom door. Hanging from the doorknob was an emerald-green-and-black lace teddy. His body tightened in response to the seductive garment.

His heart pounded and his groin throbbed with intense desire. Anticipation had become his partner, as he turned the knob and entered the room. Although Logan was certain he'd find Catherine waiting for him, certain she'd come back to him, he refused to succumb to her seduction until she made it clear she'd committed for good.

The room he entered was the stuff of fantasies. Mood lamps and candles and burning incense were scattered around the room, setting an undeniably sensual mood.

He glanced through sheer curtains hanging from the bedposts. Catherine lay waiting for him, covered by a single sheet, her pale skin glowing in the candlelight... She was the stuff of his fantasies. And all he had to do was step across her leopard print rug...

Catherine met his gaze. Determination to explain and set things right warred with the need to rush into Logan's arms.

Before she could decide, Logan had come up beside her and lowered himself onto the bed. "I

told you that rug would go well in the cottage."
He treated her to his most endearing grin and his
eyes—those cocoa-colored eyes—stared into
hers, filled with the most amazing emotions.
Honesty, sincerity and love.

"When you decide to come around, you do it
in style." He let out a long breath. "I'd counted
you out, Cat. I figured there was nothing that
would convince you we weren't a disaster waiting
to happen."

She reached a hand out to cup his cheek. "I
grew up lonely, Logan. Always waiting for my
father to come back. Relying on a mother who
wasn't ever there—not emotionally anyway, and
later on, not even physically. I was always
prepared for the worst."

"And it always happened."

She nodded.

"Even with us," he continued. "The press conference, the media frenzy…"

"Happened for the best. It showed me what I
could handle and forced me to go after what I
want." She looked him in the eye. "And I want
you."

He propped himself up on the bed and
wrapped his arms around her. A combination of
easy warmth and heated sexual need raced

through her. It was always that way with Logan, the intense mix of desire and comfort.

"You know I want you, too. But want isn't enough. Not between us."

"I know." She lay her head against his chest. The rapid beating of his heart told her he wasn't as relaxed as he appeared. Which was a good thing considering she was nowhere near composed. "At first the scandal gave me an excuse to run. Embarrassment was an excuse. And later, being without you, it made me take stock and realize I'm worthy of anything or anyone, including Logan Montgomery."

"I've known that all along." His fingers tangled in her hair, tugging with urgent insistency. "And the way you faced down the judge, I can tell you, he knows it, too." He tipped her head back to meet his gaze. "I'll spend the rest of my life making sure you never forget it."

"I love you," she murmured and met his lips for a scorching kiss, all the more heated because of the emotions involved. To her shock, her eyes filled with tears. Because she'd finally gotten everything she'd ever wanted in life—and never dared to dream of. The plastic ring would remind her, should she ever forget.

A salty drop of water slipped between their

lips. Logan lifted his head. "You're crying?" He swiped at the stray tear with his hand.

Catherine shrugged, then forced a laugh. "What can I say? I'm a sucker for a happy ending."

He held her hands tight, never wanting to let her go. "I thought you didn't believe in happily ever after."

"I didn't...until you."

"This might come as a shock to you, but I didn't believe, either." For all his posturing and attempts to convince Catherine they had a future, Logan wasn't certain he'd possessed the faith in happily ever after that he'd claimed to have.

"What changed your mind?" she asked.

"You. You're my happily ever after, Cat." He looked into her green eyes.

She rolled back onto the bed, holding out her arms for him, and whispered in her most seductive voice, "Then come home."

EPILOGUE

A SMALL BAND PLAYED in the background while the sun shone overhead, basking the beach in warmth. Catherine grabbed Logan's hand and squeezed hard. "Would you mind giving up this dance with me?" she asked.

"Are you tired?" He pulled her close, and placed his hand over her still flat stomach. "We could make excuses and go inside to lie down." A wicked grin touched his lips.

"Not at our own wedding we can't." She laughed. "Besides I'm fine. Just a little pregnant." She smiled. "I just wanted to ask someone else to dance."

His eyes narrowed. "Who?"

"Your father."

"He's here, he's drinking a glass of champagne, he's grudgingly accepting life, but that may be taking things too far."

A light gust of wind whipped her hair around

her face, bringing with it the salty smell of the ocean. "You don't think he'd want to dance with his daughter-in-law?" she asked, mock hurt in her voice.

"Of course he would. At least I think he would. Between you and my mother, he's come around. Sort of. But dancing on the beach? That may be below the judge's standards," he said wryly.

Remembering his face when they'd told Logan's father they would be married on the beach and not at the Montgomery Estate, Catherine had to agree. "He's got to realize what he's been missing in life, and twirling around the sand barefoot is one of life's grand experiences."

Logan laughed. "Okay, Cat. Do your best."

A loud shriek interrupted them and Catherine whirled around in time to see Kayla being carried off by Kane. "At least they're having a good time," she said.

"They'd have a good time anywhere they were together." Logan nuzzled her cheek. "Like us."

"Who's got Ace?" Catherine asked, using Kane's pet name for his son, Tim.

"I do."

Catherine turned to see Grace standing beside them.

Logan's sister had arrived last week and she'd been staying in Catherine's apartment in the city. Both Catherine and Logan had wanted her to stay at the beach house, but she didn't want to intrude and the mansion had been out of the question. Catherine couldn't help but notice her strained relationship with her parents, along with the longing in Grace's eyes. Like Logan, she desired more out of her family. She probably needed it more, too.

Catherine's eyes narrowed. If she could convince Grace to stick around, she could work on the entire Montgomery family dynamic. She grinned. If she could bring Judge Edgar Montgomery around with Logan, Grace couldn't be all that hard.

"What are you thinking?" Logan asked.

"How wonderful it is to have everyone together. And Grace, I was wondering if you'd consider moving back here."

The graceful, willowy blonde shook her head while reshifting Kane and Kayla's bundle in her arms. "I don't think that would work. But don't worry. I won't be a stranger."

"You'd better not, young lady."

"Hi, Gran." Logan held his arm out for Emma and gave her a loving squeeze as she kissed his cheek.

"Grace, you're my final project. Do you have any idea how difficult it was to finagle these two together?" Emma asked. "Now it's your turn. I refuse to leave this earth without seeing you happily settled down."

"You're too healthy to go anywhere just yet," Grace told her.

"You never know. Now Logan, just look how perfect she looks with the baby in her arms."

Grace, who had been holding Ace with comfort and ease, shifted uncomfortably and the little guy let out a squeal of displeasure.

Logan laughed. "I'll take him."

His sister handed him over. "Stay out of my life, Gran."

Catherine laughed. They'd been down this road before.

Emma shook her head. "I think a trip to New York City is in order, don't you, Catherine? I haven't been there in ages and, of course, my granddaughter couldn't possibly turn me away."

Grace stiffened, but like Logan, the love in her expression shone through despite her displeasure with Emma's meddling ways. "My apartment is small, Gran."

"Any cute neighbors?"

Logan laughed and grabbed for Catherine's

elbow, leading her away. "We've had our turn. Let Grace handle Emma now."

"You're bad, Logan."

"But you love me just the same."

She settled her lips over his for a deep, mind-drugging kiss. "You know I do." The baby cooed in his arms and Catherine smiled. She'd have one of her own in less than nine months. Hers and Logan's.

"And I love you."

"Then let me go dance with your father." She gestured to where Logan's parents stood stiffly overlooking the beach, his father in a suit, his mother, at least, in a comfortable sundress. And bare feet. Catherine laughed. Of all the things she hadn't expected, his mother's approval had been it. Cat actually enjoyed spending time with her, and considering she'd been instrumental in convincing the judge to accept Logan and Catherine or lose everything, Cat felt as if she owed her.

"Go ahead," Logan said. "But I'll be waiting for you."

Just as each of them had been waiting for each other. All their lives.